The Gallows Gang

After escaping en route to their appointment with the gallows, eight condemned men led by Javier Rodriguez blazed a trail of destruction. Wherever they went, the Gallows Gang left behind swinging bodies as a reminder of the fate they had avoided.

Four men set out to bring them to justice, but the prison guard Shackleton Frost and Marshal Kurt McLynn both blamed the other for the prisoners having escaped. All they could agree on is that they didn't trust Nathaniel McBain. Wrongly condemned himself, Nathaniel knows the Gallows Gang hold the key to proving his innocence. None of them knew what demons drove the enigmatic man known only as The Preacher.

Can this mismatched group put aside their personal feuds for long enough to end the Gallows Gang's reign of terror?

The Gallows Gang

I.J. Parnham

A Black Horse Western

ROBERT HALE · LONDON

© I.J. Parnham 2008
First published in Great Britain 2008

ISBN 978-0-7090-8677-2

Robert Hale Limited
Clerkenwell House
Clerkenwell Green
London EC1R 0HT

www.halebooks.com

Typeset by
Derek Doyle & Associates, Shaw Heath
Printed and bound in Great Britain by
CPI Antony Rowe, Wiltshire

CHAPTER 1

'Take the knife,' Mitch Cartwright said, 'before the guards see it.'

Nathaniel McBain considered the sharpened length of metal wrapped in cloth, which was lying at the bottom of the water bucket. Temptation made his heart beat faster and his fingers twitch, but he shook his head.

'I get out in five days,' he said. 'I'd be a fool to join you.'

'You'll get out in five minutes if you join us.'

'I know, but give it to Ramsey. He's got another seven years.' Nathaniel held Mitch's gaze for a moment. 'And good luck.'

Mitch nodded, then moved on down the line to Ramsey Carr, who wasted no time in thrusting his hands into the bucket and scooping out a handful of water to drink.

He drank slowly with his head bowed, watching the nearest prison guard, who wasn't paying the ' process of watering the prisoners too much atten-tion. So he scooped out a second handful to splash

5

on his face, but this time he drew out the makeshift knife.

While Mitch moved on to Turner Jackson, the third man in their small detail, Ramsey wrapped a large hand around the knife, then clutched the bunched hand to his chest, sighing with relief. He'd waited for years to get a weapon in his grasp and now his future was in his own hands again, his contented expression said.

So far the breakout from Beaver Ridge jail was going as planned.

Last month Hiram Deeds, the head guard in the quarry – and also the least trustworthy guard, had been bribed to look the other way when a hole had been blasted out to give the prisoners access to a new rock seam.

Mitch Cartwright had purloined two sticks of dynamite, but not for long. Something that dangerous going missing had been noticed within minutes and it had taken only another ten minutes to locate the missing sticks, but Mitch hadn't been disappointed.

The dynamite hadn't been his target.

The sticks had been stored in a box that had a metal rim around the edges and it was the metal that he had wanted. So while the guards were frantically searching for the dynamite he'd broken up the box and distributed it amongst the prisoners.

Then the work had begun. Working late at night, slowly and secretly, the pieces had been shaped then sharpened. Using bare hands and having only the stone walls to scrape against, it had taken a month to get them into the right shape but eventually a dozen sharp knives had resulted.

Now, what was planned to be the largest ever breakout from Beaver Ridge jail was approaching its crucial final stage in the quarry, the nearest point in the jail to the outside world. Mitch had distributed the knives during a break in the daily grind of rock-breaking, and now the distraction was about to start.

'You not coming, then?' Ramsey said, making his way over to Nathaniel now that the short break was over.

'No,' Nathaniel said as they turned away to face the heap of rocks on which they'd been working. 'Like I've been saying, once I get out of here I'll make sure I never end up in a place like this again. I'll just stay back when it happens.'

Ramsey nodded. 'And you, Turner?'

Turner didn't meet Ramsey's eye as he shuffled round to head back to the rock face, making Ramsey grunt his question again. This time Turner did look at him, but he shook his head.

'I ain't going either,' he murmured.

Ramsey looked around. No guard was close enough to hear them as the prisoners dispersed to their positions at the slowest pace that wouldn't invite retribution, as if everything was normal.

'But you've got life,' Ramsey said, his eyes opening wide with astonishment. 'This is your only hope of tasting freedom again.'

'It ain't. I've been working on Hiram Deeds, telling him a tale about a hidden stash of gold I have

7

on the outside. He says he'll get me out of here. I reckon I'll take my chances with him.'

Ramsey's eyes opened even wider before he shot an amused glance at Nathaniel, who registered his bemusement with a low whistle. Hiram Deeds was less reliable with his promises than the average prisoner was.

'I wouldn't believe anything he says,' Nathaniel said. 'That man is—'

'Move along there,' the strident voice of their guard demanded from behind them. 'Your free time is over. Get back to work.'

The three men moved towards their rock-hammers ready to begin the process of converting large rocks into small rocks, but they moved slowly, waiting. . . .

A loud oath-filled shout went up from the other side of the quarry.

The three men turned, their quick motions making them appear shocked. Up the slope on the other side of the quarry two prisoners, Casey Dawson and Swift Tate, were pushing each other while shouting taunts.

Fights were common and often the guards let them run their course, figuring that working off steam did everyone some good, and sure enough nobody moved to break them up.

Swift and Casey grabbed each other and after a brief skirmish the larger prisoner, Casey, grounded Swift with a flailing punch to the nose. Then he proceeded to kick him viciously and repeatedly in the ribs, making him rise with every blow.

'That's enough,' their guard said after the fourth blow, advancing on them.

Seemingly appeased Casey delivered one last kick, then turned on his heel and made his way back to his position. But the fallen Swift hadn't had enough. He rolled to his knees, rubbed his bruised ribs, then ran for his rock-hammer.

Casey heard him rise and turned to see his opponent charging at him with the hammer raised high above his head, ready to deliver a pulverizing blow.

He threw himself to the side, narrowly avoiding the descending hammer, which crashed into the ground, sending rock slivers scything in all directions. Then, with another aggrieved grunt, Swift raised the hammer again.

By now the fight had got everyone's attention.

'Get him!' one prisoner shouted.

'Casey stole from me too,' another shouted. 'Crush him!'

Within seconds the quarry was alive with motion as the prisoners scurried towards the fight.

Nathaniel stayed back as did Turner, and Ramsey took advantage of their desire to keep out of this by staying with them so he could remain close to their guard.

Around the quarry the guards shot glances towards the quarry rim where Hiram Deeds sat in his imperious position, asking whether they should step in or let Swift and Casey settle their differences. But with Swift wielding a ten-pound hammer, even a man like Hiram had an easy decision to make.

'Enough!' he roared, his voice echoing.

That demand didn't deter the prisoners from milling in, so he fired into the air. The prisoners ignored him, instead forming a circle around Swift and Casey and urging Swift to bury the hammer in Casey's head.

Inside the circle Swift advanced on Casey with measured intent, so Hiram shouted out for five guards to break up the circle and separate the two fighting prisoners, pointing at the men he'd selected to do the task.

One of those men was the guard looking after Nathaniel's group. After muttering a quick order to the nearest guard to take over the duty of looking after them, he moved off.

'Wait,' Turner said, stepping forward.

'Be quiet,' the guard muttered, not breaking his stride.

'But you've got to. I promised Hiram.'

While Nathaniel and Ramsey shot surprised looks at him, then at each other, wondering if this was part of the plan, the guard turned.

'Promised him what?'

'That I'd keep him informed.' Turner looked up towards Hiram, then shot an ashamed glance at Nathaniel and Ramsey. 'This fight ain't what it seems. It's a—'

Turner didn't get to complete what was clearly going to be a foolhardy attempt to curry favour with Hiram Deeds by selling everyone out, because

Ramsey let out a great roar, then charged at him. He wrapped a large arm around his waist and carried him back several paces.

Nathaniel had resolved to avoid getting involved, but Turner's duplicity had enraged him too. He joined Ramsey in wrestling Turner to the ground. While Ramsey slapped a hand over his mouth, Nathaniel pinned him down.

But the damage had already been done.

'The fight's a trap!' the guard shouted.

Around the quarry everyone froze. None of the guards was close to the prisoners, as they needed to be when the prisoners revealed their hidden knives. With the element of surprise gone, the circle broke up and the prisoners ran towards their nearest targets.

In response the alerted guards backed away while the armed ones drew their guns.

Ramsey released his grip of Turner's head, aiming to run at the guard who had alerted everyone, but Turner threw out a hand and grabbed his arm, dragging him down.

As a hubbub of shouting and gunfire rose around him Nathaniel struggled to keep Turner held down, but with him wriggling madly, all three men went sprawling, their frantic movements sending them tumbling down the side of the quarry. They rolled over each other, coming to an entangled halt twenty feet further down the slope.

Nathaniel lay for a moment, winded, then raised himself to see that the attempted breakout had ended almost before it had got started.

Several guards were lying on their backs clutching stab wounds, and he counted the bodies of at least three shot prisoners. Most of the other prisoners were kneeling with their hands on their heads. The few free ones, brandishing knives, were nowhere near their target guards and were being shouted at to drop their weapons or be shot.

A guard was making his way purposefully towards them, so Nathaniel pre-empted his demand by kneeling and putting his hands on his head. He looked at Ramsey to see if he'd done the same, but only the double-crossing Turner was sitting up and he was staring down at Ramsey.

Nathaniel followed his gaze to see that Ramsey was lying on his back with his eyes glazed and lifeless, his neck arched backwards, baring his bloody throat. The knife that he'd waited for so long to get his hands on stuck upwards from his jugular, blood pooling up around it.

'Step away from him,' the guard said.

'It was an accident,' Turner said.

'Sure was,' Nathaniel said.

The guard sneered with disbelief as he looked at Nathaniel.

'I saw what happened and that weren't no accident.' He snorted. 'And to think you only had five days before you got freedom. Now, you've got about five days before you get the gallows.'

CHAPTER 2

'I reckon it'd be easier to just hang Javier Rodriguez here in Beaver Ridge,' Shackleton Frost said.

Marshal Kurt McLynn nodded. 'It would, but Mayor Maxwell reckons the townsfolk of Bear Creek suffered plenty at the hands of the Rodriguez brothers and they deserve better than to just hear Javier got hung in some jail over two hundred miles away. And now that the mayor's invited the state governor to come and see how he deals with outlaws, it's all become bigger than just one man and one execution.'

'I know that, but ten men is a lot of manpower to transport one man.'

Kurt sat back in his chair and with a raised foot pushed himself away from the desk – *my* desk, Shackleton couldn't help but note.

Ever since the governor of Beaver Ridge jail, Wes Bradbury, had appointed a US Marshal to oversee the task of delivering the outlaw Javier Rodriguez to his demise, a confrontation had been inevitable. To

Shackleton's way of thinking, the meeting to discuss the task's arrangements was as good a time as any.

For the last three years Shackleton and his small and trusted detail of two men had escorted prisoners from the small town jailhouses to Beaver Ridge. Never once had a prisoner escaped *en route*, and Shackleton was rightly proud of that record.

Even when Marshal Kurt McLynn had captured Javier, the most dangerous of the notorious Rodriguez brothers, Shackleton's team had taken him from Bear Creek to Beaver Ridge without trouble. But now Javier's final appeal had failed and a very public and political appointment with the gallows awaited him.

To ensure that he reached Bear Creek without mishaps Governor Bradbury had decided, despite Shackleton's record, that he wasn't capable enough for the job and so he'd hired the man who had brought Javier Rodriguez to justice.

So far, Kurt and Shackleton had agreed on only one thing – they didn't like each other.

'You saying I can do it with fewer men?' Kurt asked. 'Three, for instance?'

Shackleton smiled as Kurt cut straight to the heart of his concern.

'For the last three years three men have got the job done.'

'Except this time everyone knows Javier's moving on, so if Pablo wants to save his brother, he'll have to do it between here and Bear Creek.'

'Yeah, but last time everyone knew Javier was

14

coming here *and* the townsfolk were baying for a lynching. So I took him away in the middle of the night, then used the trails nobody would expect, travelling only at night. I got him here. . . .'

Shackleton let the rest of his comment go unsaid, partly because he didn't need to say it, but mainly because he was losing the will to continue with this argument. He'd had the same debate with Governor Bradbury when he'd told him the bad news. Then he'd been unable to convince him that a small experienced detail who knew the area had a greater chance of success than a large detail putting on a deliberate show of strength.

Kurt's sneer suggested he'd never convince *him* of that, either.

'You're wasting your breath, Shackleton. Governor Bradbury hired me, so if you want to be involved you'll have to put your personal feelings aside.' Kurt cocked his head to one side. 'Should I find someone else?'

'No,' Shackleton said, then clenched his teeth.

For nearly a minute Kurt stared at him while rocking back and forth in his chair, reinforcing his command and Shackleton's subordinate status; then he softened his expression and spread his hands.

'If it helps, I can put your mind at rest on one matter.' Kurt leaned forward to take a sheet of paper from the desk. He held it out. 'I won't use ten men to guard one. We're giving Javier some company on the gallows. I'm taking at least seven other prisoners to Bear Creek.'

Shackleton took the paper and read down the list of names. The failed breakout had resulted in the deaths of two guards followed by an ongoing series of brief and merciless trials.

'For this many men we'll need a cage and that'll mean we'll have to stay on the well-travelled route along Devil's Canyon. That'll make it certain that everyone, including Pablo Rodriguez, will know exactly where we'll be.'

Kurt chuckled. 'I believe a public show of strength requires it.'

Shackleton frowned, irritated now that Kurt had converted the arrangements for this prisoner movement into the complete opposite of everything that had worked for him in the past. Then he narrowed his eyes.

'You're hoping Pablo *will* try something, aren't you? You want to be known as the man who got both the Rodriguez brothers.'

'The thought had crossed my mind.' Kurt raised his eyebrows in an invitation to Shackleton to join him in finding the idea enticing.

But Shackleton's job was purely to transport prisoners and he could see nothing to smile about.

'In that case,' he said, 'perhaps ten men might not be enough.'

'My thoughts exactly.' Kurt reached over to another list. 'I've been reviewing the details of the men here and comparing them to the men you recommended. There are some surprising omissions.'

Shackleton took the second list. The top name made him wince.

'Hiram Deeds!' he spluttered.

'Why not? His information let the governor know a breakout was being planned. It's men like him that I need.'

'Hiram Deeds only got that information by taking bribes. He's the biggest double-crossing snake you'll ever find on this side of the jailhouse bars.' Shackleton shook his head. 'If you're thinking of putting him on the detail, I want nothing to do with this.'

'That's fine with me, Shackleton, because I like men like Hiram who don't question my orders.' Kurt smirked. 'And I'm starting to think he'd be a better man to do your job.'

'Get out there, Nathaniel McBain,' the guard said, gesturing to the door. 'You've got an appointment with a short rope.'

Nathaniel pushed himself off his cot and got to his feet. Hope that common sense would prevail made sweat break out on his brow, but he still trudged out of the cell, resigned to what was about to happen.

The other prisoners in this secure part of the jail behind the courtroom glared at him from their own cells. Most had already been tried for their part in the attempted breakout, which explained their surly looks, but not why several men ran to the front of their cells to shout taunts and spit at him.

By the time Nathaniel reached the door a cacophony of noise accompanied him, making the guard push him through the door then go back in to quell the rising disquiet.

Nathaniel found himself unguarded in a short corridor: not that freedom here would help him. The only other door led to the jail courtroom.

Turner Jackson was already standing in the corridor, but he didn't look up to acknowledge him. Nathaniel soon saw the reason for his sullen attitude. Bruises darkened his face and he stood with a stiff posture as if that beating had spread elsewhere.

'They treat you badly?' Nathaniel asked.

'It wasn't the guards,' Turner murmured. 'They put me in with two other prisoners. Everyone's looking for a scapegoat.'

'Can you blame them? You did warn the guard.' Nathaniel snorted as he looked Turner up and down, feeling a twinge of sympathy for him. He might have sold everyone out, but even if he avoided the gallows, Turner's life term was sure to be a short and painful one. 'I hope for your sake that Hiram Deeds delivers on his promises.'

Turner shuffled unhappily from foot to foot, acknowledging this was unlikely, then raised his chin defiantly.

'You ain't got nothing to gloat about, Nathaniel. We were on the same detail.'

Nathaniel nodded. 'So that's why they were all shouting at me. They think I'm as guilty as you are.'

'Yeah. So you'd better hope you don't get left alone with anyone, either.'

'I've got nothing to fear. I know the truth about what happened.' Nathaniel sighed. 'And for that matter, telling the truth in there is the only thing that can save us from the gallows.'

Turner's sneer suggested he thought this was an even more unlikely prospect than Hiram Deeds helping him.

Then they both waited in pensive silence for the guard to return and take them to the courtroom where they faced the visiting judge along with Governor Bradbury and Hiram Deeds. The only witnesses were guards, adding further weight to Turner's belief that this would turn out badly.

Judge Matthews heard the testimony of the guard who had separated them, his story being that they had silenced Ramsey Carr to settle an old grudge before they escaped. The judge grunted with satisfaction on hearing this summation of events, then turned to Nathaniel with the bored air of a man going through the formalities.

'Nathaniel McBain,' he said, 'serving seven years for numerous robberies and misdemeanours, but never with violence. It would appear your time in here has helped you develop a killing streak.'

'It's the opposite,' Nathaniel said, standing tall as he spoke his mind honestly. 'I took to thieving only because I was hungry and misguided, but I know now I did wrong and the regime here has changed me. When I get out of here I plan to work hard and stay out of trouble.'

The courtroom echoed to subdued snorts of derision. Judge Matthews waited with his chin resting on an upturned hand until the commotion had quietened down before replying.

'Nathaniel McBain, I've been subjected to an endless litany of lies over the last two days and I'm in no mood for any more.' He leaned forward. 'You say you planned to stay out of trouble and yet you killed a man.'

'I didn't. It was an accident. I . . .' Nathaniel noted that Judge Matthews was tapping his fingers on his desk with exasperation. The prisoner code of conduct was never to sell out your fellow prisoner, and Nathaniel found that he couldn't do it even when that other prisoner was Turner Jackson. 'I admit we were fighting, but it weren't to settle no grudge. It was another matter.'

Judge Matthews snorted. 'And then you planned to escape?'

Nathaniel took a deep breath. In thinking through how he would explain away the incident, he had only one indisputable fact that would help him and now was, he felt, as good a time as any to mention it.

'I wasn't planning on escaping. I only had five days of my sentence left to serve. I plan to avoid jail for the rest of my life, so I'd have been foolish to risk everything by attempting to escape, wouldn't I?'

This declaration had the desired effect of making Judge Matthews raise his eyebrows and show some interest in proceedings for the first time.

'Perhaps you would,' he said, 'although that still

leaves the matter of you fighting with another prisoner for a reason you are not prepared to divulge.'

'And I'll take my punishment for that, but I didn't kill Ramsey and I wasn't trying to escape.'

Judge Matthews leaned towards Governor Bradbury and engaged in a whispered conversation, then looked at Nathaniel with his head still bowed.

'And who was holding the knife?'

'I don't know,' Nathaniel said, 'but it wasn't me.'

He glanced at Turner, but Turner was staring at the floor and gave no sign that he had heard his comment.

'So your story is that Turner killed Ramsey?'

'I didn't say that!' Nathaniel said, taking a pace forward. 'I just meant—'

'Silence!' Judge Matthews glared at him until he took a pace backwards, then turned his gaze on to Turner. 'And what's your story, Turner Jackson, serving life for bank robbery, manslaughter, to detail just the top two items on your very long list of crimes?'

Turner kept staring at the floor until a guard nudged him, making him raise his head. He lifted a manacled hand to rub his chest, wincing, then looked around the courtroom, taking in the row of hostile witnesses.

Then he dropped to his knees, raised his hands in a pleading gesture, and bleated out his story.

'It was Nathaniel,' he screeched. 'He held the knife. He killed Ramsey. He—'

'You double-crossing . . .' Nathaniel said then swung round to Turner, aiming to finish the job that

21

the other prisoners had started.

He only managed to swing back a manacled hand, aiming to strike Turner across his lying mouth before a guard stepped in and clubbed the back of his head, knocking him to the floor.

He lay stunned while Turner blurted out a story that started with Nathaniel having just shown everyone how bad a temper he had. Then it went on to agree with the only other witness's version of events, except he added the detail that Nathaniel had buried the knife in Ramsey's throat.

By the time his tale had ended and Nathaniel had been dragged to his feet Judge Matthews was consulting with Governor Bradbury. Then he turned to the prisoners, his eyes lively, although Nathaniel reckoned that that was only because this was the last trial of the day.

'The punishment for a prisoner who kills another is the gallows,' he said. 'A man *was* killed and so, based on the testimony I have heard, I have to decide whether one of you should hang, or both.'

'I'm innocent,' Nathaniel said. 'Everything Turner said was a lie.'

'May the grace of the Lord Jesus be with God's people,' Judge Matthews said, ignoring Nathaniel's plea as he looked at Turner, then turned his gaze on to Nathaniel. He raised his gavel.

CHAPTER 3

'Take the men out of the cage two at a time,' Hiram Deeds ordered. 'Each group gets three minutes.'

Nathaniel had been trying to let the gathering darkness and the steady motion of the cage rock him into sleep, but it had only lulled him into a forlorn torpor. Now that they had stopped he sat hunched in the far corner of the mobile cage, watching Marshal Kurt McLynn and most of the guards disperse to take up widespread defensive positions before Hiram unlocked the cage.

Ten prisoners were in the cage, chained and attached to the bars in pairs, and his fellow captives on the two-day journey to Bear Creek all had the same blank-eyed stare as he had as they awaited the inevitable.

Nathaniel sat beside a sour-faced Mitch Cartwright, the prisoner who had handed out the knives and who had been one of the few men to get out of the quarry before being brought down.

Eight of the captives were men sentenced to the

gallows for their part in the breakout, including Turner Jackson, who sat at the opposite end of the cage to Nathaniel.

One of the few pleasures left to Nathaniel was to catch Turner's eye occasionally and snarl, letting him know that his duplicity had earned him nothing but the worst possible fate. So when Turner had been freed from the bars and had happened to glance at him before standing, Nathaniel glared back and bared his teeth, making Turner turn away.

Turner had the dubious honour of being manacled to Javier Rodriguez, who, under the traditional prison hierarchy, was treated with some deference by the other prisoners. Hiram mockingly picked up on that deference and gave a short bow as Javier stepped down from the cage.

Nobody paid deference to the only other prisoner not to have been sentenced because of the breakout. This sombre man was tall and painfully thin, and had features so gaunt they were almost skull-like. He was known only as The Preacher. He sat opposite Javier, his hands raised as high as he could get them and his head lowered while he muttered to himself, presumably in prayer.

What his crimes were Nathaniel didn't know, but the fight to avoid sitting beside him when they'd been loaded into the cage suggested that, to have worried these men, it had to have been something terrible.

When Turner and Javier had taken care of their absolutions, this being the only chance they'd get before being settled down for the night, the next two prisoners made their way out.

Mitch and Nathaniel would be the next to leave, so Nathaniel stretched his cramped limbs while looking around. They'd been riding along the rim of Devil's Canyon and had stopped so close to the edge he could see down into the canyon to the winding blue ribbon that was the river at the bottom.

He stared at the water, enjoying what would probably be one of his last pleasant sights, until his turn came. Then, with an uncomfortable rattling of chains as he and Mitch tried to establish a walking rhythm, they headed down the cage, but Nathaniel stopped beside Turner.

'As long as they string you up first and I get to see your lying body,' Nathaniel said, 'I'll die a happy man.'

Turner didn't meet his eye as he squirmed uncomfortably on the base of the cage. Nathaniel resisted the urge to kick him, reckoning he might get a better chance to work off his anger on him later, then he left the cage.

'Bushes over there,' Hiram said, pointing, 'and be quick.'

Nathaniel and Mitch made their way over, but Mitch dawdled, making every pace a fight.

'Get into step,' Nathaniel said.

'Ain't got nothing in step with you,' Mitch grumbled.

Nathaniel sighed. 'You don't believe those rumours Turner started that it's my fault it all went wrong, do you?'

'Sure do. Turner told us everything. How you sold us out to Hiram Deeds. How you sounded the alarm. How you killed Ramsey when he tried to stop you.'

Nathaniel shook his head. 'That's not the way it was. Turner was the one who . . .'

Nathaniel saw the scepticism in Mitch's eyes, so he gave up attempting to explain himself. Once rumours became widespread they were accepted as fact and nobody would listen to the truth. Not that it mattered this close to the gallows.

He turned away from Mitch, aiming to drop his pants first, but then a whipping blow to the side of his head with the loop of chain that connected them sent him face first into the dirt.

A mixture of his fall and the shared manacles dragged Mitch down on top of him. He tried to buck him away but Mitch had a tight grip on the chain and he dragged it round Nathaniel's neck, then drew back, choking him.

Nathaniel threw his hands to his neck and grabbed the cold metal, but he couldn't tear it away from his neck to let him breathe. So he lunged for Mitch's hands, but the man's bunched fists were like iron.

Slowly Mitch twisted the chain, tightening it even more.

Motes of light and darkness flitted across Nathaniel's vision as he fought for the air he couldn't gulp in. Then footfalls approached, followed by a thud. Mitch's hold slipped away, letting Nathaniel roll on to his side, gasping.

Then the guards beat Mitch and they even landed a few blows on Nathaniel for good measure. Afterwards they pulled both men to their feet and dragged them back to the cage.

'Nobody gets out now,' Hiram said. 'You'll all just have to stink up the cage.'

'Hey,' Mitch whined when they reached the door. 'I don't want to spend the rest of my life chained to this double-crosser.'

The guard ignored him and moved to push him into the cage, but Hiram stopped him with a raised hand.

'Wait,' he said. 'We don't want no trouble tonight. Chain him to someone else.'

'Who?' the guard asked. 'Nobody wants to sit beside the man who got them all put in there.'

As Hiram considered the prisoners, Turner muttered that Mitch was right about Nathaniel being a double-crosser and this encouraged most of the men to grunt that they didn't want to be chained to him either.

Hiram's gaze stopped when it reached the last man in the cage. He smiled.

'Teach him a lesson for selling everyone out,' he said. 'Manacle him to The Preacher.'

'Obliged,' Mitch shouted, and the order gathered grunts of approval from the other prisoners.

'And then I want no more trouble from in here,' Hiram snapped, pointing at each prisoner in turn. 'I've brought dynamite along. At the first sign of

27

trouble I'll blow you all to hell.'

In short order they removed Nathaniel's manacles and transferred him to sit beside The Preacher. His new companion didn't stop his steady muttering to himself, leaving Nathaniel to wonder why this was such a punishment.

Once he was sitting, Turner caught his eye from the other side of the cage.

'If Mitch can't get you,' he said, 'at least I can get to watch you enjoying your time with The Preacher.'

'He ain't so bad after suffering Mitch's company,' Nathaniel said, 'and your lies.'

'You'll have changed your mind by morning.' Turner laughed. 'Provided The Preacher doesn't eat you in the night.'

'I reckon this is the best position,' Marshal Kurt McLynn said, looking over Shackleton Frost's shoulder at the cage 400 yards ahead of and below them.

Shackleton drew back from the edge of the ridge and shook his head.

'I don't agree,' he said. 'We should be nearer to the cage and you need other men scouting around.'

Kurt laughed when he noted Shackleton's grim expression.

'Still questioning my orders, I see. Will you stop whining if Pablo Rodriguez does show and I bring him to justice?'

'Nope. I don't care about him. I guard prisoners and all I care about is discharging my duty.'

'*My* duty,' Kurt said. '*Your* duty is to do what I say,

without questioning me.'

'Yes, *sir*,' Shackleton snapped. 'And what are my orders now, sir?'

Kurt stared at Shackleton for several seconds to ensure he knew he'd noticed his sarcasm, then he gestured down the ridge.

'Demonstrate that local knowledge you're so proud of. Decide on the direction Pablo is most likely to come from, then lie in wait for him. If you guess right, capture him and hold him until I arrive.'

Shackleton nodded, then turned to go, but he'd had to swallow a lot of pride over the last few days to stay involved with this mission and the urge to speak his mind became too great. He turned back.

'Before I go, I'll say this – you're a fool.' This act of open defiance made the rest of Kurt's men look up in shock. 'We could have got Javier Rodriguez to Bear Creek without any trouble if we'd done this my way, but riding openly down Devil's Canyon is inviting disaster, and hiring Hiram Deeds was utter madness.'

Shackleton could have gone on to detail everything Kurt had done wrong in setting up this mission, but Kurt's sneer said it'd fall on deaf ears, so he turned away, giving the marshal no chance for a retort. Now he welcomed the opportunity to spend time with the two-man team he'd worked with for the last three years.

With his head down he snaked along the top of the ridge to join Barney Clarke and Elwood Brown.

The two men noted Shackleton's firm-jawed

29

expression and each cast a smiling glance at the other, acknowledging their own thoughts about Kurt and his methods. Then they settled down to await darkness.

An hour later they made their move.

Elwood pointed out their destination and route in a silent and quick manner that only people who have worked together for years could understand.

Then they made their way down from the ridge and into a winding gully that came out 400 yards from the edge of the canyon and slightly further away from the cage. There, a bright fire was now lighting up a semicircle a hundred yards wide.

Flickering light even played along the rim of the other side of the canyon a quarter-mile away.

Elwood and Barney murmured their disapproval of the lack of a guarded fire, but Shackleton said nothing. They had both heard enough of his complaints.

Now they just had to wait to see if Pablo would show. As the northern route to this point had plenty of cover, whereas the southern route was more open, Elwood judged he'd pass them here.

'Do you reckon he'll come?' Shackleton asked.

'Ain't got a clue,' Barney said, while Elwood gave the question more careful consideration.

'If I were Pablo and I knew that double-crossing snake Hiram Deeds was looking after the cage, I'd . . .' Elwood looked around then lowered his voice. 'I'd already be here.'

Shackleton flinched, not having expected this

answer. He then followed Elwood's gaze to look at the ridge, then along the route that Elwood indicated with an outstretched finger. He nodded, seeing what Elwood had noted.

Although the fire was bright enough to appear to have been carelessly situated, a large boulder could be seen between the fire and the cage; it prevented the prisoners from getting any of the warmth and light, and also ensured that were shrouded in darkness. Between the edge of the canyon and the ridge there was 400 yards of open space, but there were enough mounds and hollows to mean that long stretches of the ground were in shadow.

'So Hiram is doing precisely what I tried to warn Kurt about,' Shackleton murmured, aghast.

'Yup. He's lit up the area to let us all see that everything is fine. Except, come the morning, the cage will be one prisoner short.'

'Or will have one prisoner more if I have anything to do with it.'

'There is no dark place,' The Preacher muttered to himself, 'no deep shadow, where evildoers can hide, Job thirty-four, verse twenty-two.'

The Preacher was now talking loudly enough for Nathaniel to hear him, not that he cared to spend the night listening to an endless series of Bible quotations. Although, mindful of the man's reputation, he'd decided not to antagonize him by telling him to be quiet.

Around the cage rasping snores indicated that

most of the prisoners were asleep. When he abandoned his own attempt to sleep and opened his eyes he saw that, opposite him, Turner Jackson was asleep but Javier Rodriguez was awake. Javier's eyes reflected the limited light as they darted around following the guards on their regular patrol.

The tense yet poised way he sat leaning back against the bars suggested he hadn't given up hope of escape. That made Nathaniel wonder whether something might happen tonight that could give him a chance to escape too.

The first hint that something really was amiss came when Nathaniel heard a thud nearby, then the sound of a large object being dragged along.

Javier's eyes followed the motion of whoever was doing the dragging. When that man came into Nathaniel's view he saw that Hiram Deeds was dragging an unconscious guard towards the large boulder that stood between them and the fire.

Then Hiram made his stealthy way towards them, holding a bunched set of keys.

Nathaniel closed his eyes to slits and let his mouth fall open as if he were snoozing. He watched Hiram open the cage door in a slow way that ensured it didn't creak and awaken the prisoners.

Hiram appraised The Preacher, but he continued to babble, showing no interest in the proceedings, as usual. Then he leaned over to Javier and passed him a key.

Javier settled back and considered the prisoners, assuring himself that they were all still asleep; then he looked at Turner, then at Hiram who followed his gaze. Nathaniel guessed that a silent discussion was taking place as to whether to release Turner. That discussion ended when Javier reached down to his ankle.

While carefully avoiding touching Turner's body he released his leg manacles, then drew his leg away from him. Again he waited for a few moments before he released his wrist from both Turner and the bars. Then he stood slowly and moved towards the open door.

Nathaniel waited until he raised the hand holding the key to the bars to steady himself as he climbed down. Then he lunged out with his own free hand, catching Javier's wrist. He squeezed.

He and Javier exchanged eye contact as Nathaniel conveyed with his bunched fist and flared eyes that he had the power to ensure this escape wouldn't remain a secret for long if he chose to raise the alarm.

'Take me with you,' he whispered.

CHAPTER 4

'I've worked out how Hiram will get him to Pablo,' Elwood said when he returned from his thirty minutes of scouting around.

He beckoned for Shackleton and Barney to join him. Without asking questions, they followed.

Keeping in the shadows and often crawling like snakes along the ground they inched closer to the cage, taking a circuitous route that several times doubled back almost to the place where they'd started. Shackleton couldn't see where Elwood was taking them until they were almost there.

Silently Elwood edged forward and rolled from view as he disappeared into a dried-out rill. Shackleton and Barney followed to find that the course of the rill was around three feet deep and followed a more or less straight course from the ridge to the edge of the canyon. A brief glance over the side confirmed that it emerged twenty yards from the cage.

Lying on his belly, Shackleton ran his gaze up and

down the watercourse then patted Elwood's back.

'Agreed,' he said. 'Javier could get away from the cage along here without being noticed from up on the ridge.'

'So do we get closer?'

'No. Javier won't go anywhere without passing by us, so let's see who's at the other end.'

Barney and Elwood grunted their approval of this plan. With Shackleton leading they crawled along the watercourse towards the ridge.

They'd covered 200 yards when movement ahead caught Shackleton's eye, about twenty yards ahead. He froze; the two men behind were aware enough of his movements also to halt immediately.

'Pablo, or Kurt?' Elwood whispered, crawling along to lie beside Shackleton.

'I reckon Kurt ain't the kind of man who sneaks around in the dark.'

Elwood grunted that he agreed. Then they carried on, this time moving more slowly than before, taking fifteen minutes to reach the sprawl of boulders where Shackleton had seen something move. There they waited, listening to the wind, the sounds of the guards moving around the cage. . . .

A crunch sounded as of a footfall on grit, followed by a second. Then, looming up against the night sky, a man walked to the edge of the watercourse, looking out towards the canyon. He planted his feet a few inches from Shackleton's head and stood, rocking back and forth as he stretched his cramped limbs.

From over by the canyon the faint sounds of movement sounded, perhaps giving a reason for his having come forward to investigate.

Presently the sounds petered out and so with a grunt to himself the man edged backwards a half-pace while looking around. His eyes took in the ridge above him. Then he looked to the cage and finally along the watercourse, his head swinging down as his vision lit upon the men lying beneath his feet.

Elwood was the first to react. He lunged out with a firm hand and grabbed the man's leg, then yanked it. Surprise ensured that the man didn't put up a fight and went tumbling down into the dry watercourse. thereupon all three men leapt on him and subdued him, though not before he'd emitted a screeching cry.

His alarm echoed amongst the gullies and passes of the ridge above as Barney delivered a solid blow to the man's cheek, which crashed his head against the ground, making him flop. They held on to him for a moment longer to make sure he was out cold, but by then voices were rising up around them in the dark.

Someone to their left hissed a question. Another person to their right uttered an audible demand for quiet while another said it was too late.

Thirty yards down the watercourse two men appeared, looking towards the cage.

'Is it happening?' one asked.

'I don't think so. That sounded like Jim.'

Gazing about him, the two men took in their surroundings. They couldn't help but see the four men in the watercourse. Slowly they turned towards them. Then, with a grunted exchange, they scrambled for their guns, but Shackleton's group had already drawn and they had a bead on them.

Again using the unspoken understanding of each other's intentions that didn't need spoken orders Shackleton blasted two rapid shots into the man on the left while Barney and Elwood shot a slug apiece into the one on the right.

Even before the shot men had hit the dirt they had rolled to their feet. Then, doubled-over, they ran towards the boulders from where the first man had emerged. They ducked down and peered out, awaiting developments.

'They got Charlie and Lester,' a voice cried out, now giving up all attempts to be quiet.

'Where are they?'

'I don't know.'

'It sounded as if—'

Gunfire exploded, the sounds of the rapid shots echoing all around them, and the gunfire itself was just as wild and splayed.

Shackleton judged that Kurt's men were shooting from their various hiding-places along the ridge. They were firing blind with little idea as to where their targets were. So the shots were peppering over a range that went from fifty yards into the flat area to a point high up on the ridge.

'There must be more men out there than we thought,' someone shouted. 'We're surrounded.'

'To the horses!'

'What about Javier?'

'Later!'

Then rapid footfalls sounded, receding into the darkness, followed by the sounds of around ten men mounting up.

'We going after 'em?' Barney asked, then ducked as a stray bullet tore into the ground a few feet to his side.

'Those were our orders,' Shackleton said, 'and we ain't the ones in charge no more.'

'I know,' Elwood said unhappily as the riders hurried into sight and initiated a ferocious burst of gunfire from numerous directions along the ridge. 'We'd have avoided all this.'

'Pablo's a fool,' Hiram Deeds said as the gunfire echoed. 'He's been seen.'

As the gunfire roused the prisoners from their slumbers he yanked Javier outside and slammed the cage door in Nathaniel's face.

'That means you've failed,' Javier Rodriguez muttered, facing Hiram.

'I haven't. Just slip away like I planned while I take care of things here.'

Hiram reached into his jacket and when his hand emerged he was brandishing a stick of dynamite.

'What you doing with that?' Javier demanded.

'What do you think I'm doing?' Hiram snapped. 'I'm blowing up the cage and sending it down into the canyon. Then nobody will be able to work out if you were in there or not.'

Nathaniel was surprised to see that Javier, a man

who was supposedly utterly ruthless, balked at this plan.

Slowly, Javier paced up to Hiram. He glanced down at the stick, then grunted with anger. He batted it away with one hand while lunging for Hiram's holster with the other. Before Hiram could react the gun was in Javier's hand and he had twirled it round in his grip.

Gunfire roared as Javier blasted a slug into Hiram's guts at point-blank range, making him fold over and slump to the ground.

Then Javier dropped to one knee. Within seconds three guards came running to investigate, but three crisp shots rang out as Javier peppered lead across them.

Even before the bodies had stopped twitching, Javier had ripped the keys from Hiram's hand.

Then he collected guns from the two nearest guards and turned to the cage to face the prisoners. They were now all awake and they considered him through the bars with a mixture of concern (presumably because most had heard Hiram's plan), and hope.

Javier Rodriguez wasted no time in letting them know their fate.

'I have the keys,' he said, holding them high. 'I can either leave you for the gallows, or you can join me. You might not live for long, but I can promise you we'll blaze a trail that people will talk about for a thousand years, and when you do die, you'll die as free men.'

The echoing cheer gave Javier all the answers he needed. He hurried to the cage and passed the manacle key through the bars while he opened the cage door.

Nathaniel watched proceedings quietly as the key got passed from hand to hand, but when it reached the last prisoner before him, Mitch Cartwright spoke up.

'Don't give it to him,' he said. 'That double-crosser ain't coming with us.'

'What Turner said about me was a lie,' Nathaniel said, as Mitch slipped out of the cage, leaving him and The Preacher the only prisoners left inside.

'It sure wasn't,' Mitch said, smirking. 'But don't worry. When we've gone The Preacher might forgive you, provided he doesn't get hungry first.'

Several prisoners snorted a laugh, agreeing with Mitch's plan to leave him, but Turner pushed Mitch aside and paced up to the cage.

'I have a better idea,' he said, holding Hiram's stick of dynamite high. 'Hiram was going to blow up the cage to hide what he did here. I reckon we should still do that, but with our double-crosser inside.'

This suggestion made Nathaniel swirl round and shake the bars.

'Someone listen to me!' he demanded. 'You have to listen to the truth about Turner.'

Everyone ignored him and the few who did react grunted their support for Turner's plan.

So Mitch checked that Nathaniel's chains still

secured him to the bars while Turner lit the fuse. Then he pushed the stick through the bars at the opposite end of the cage to where Nathaniel sat. It rolled only a few feet in. He caught Nathaniel's eye.

'It looks as if I'm the one,' he said, grinning, 'who gets to see you die.'

Then he ran back to the group, gibbering with delight.

'Now move on out,' Javier said with an overhead gesture. 'We need to be as far away as possible by the time that blast lights up Devil's Canyon.'

Nathaniel ignored the prisoners' departure as he strained, but the chain that secured his hand to The Preacher's was short and he could move himself only a few feet nearer to the fizzing dynamite. His straining tugged The Preacher back and forth, but his efforts didn't rouse him or stop his steady murmuring.

'We have to do something,' Nathaniel shouted at him, 'or the blast will blow us both to pieces in about two minutes.'

The Preacher's only response was to clutch his hands more tightly together and raise his voice to a strident tone.

'Blessed are those who are persecuted because of righteousness,' he intoned, 'for theirs is the kingdom of heaven, Matthew five, verse ten.'

CHAPTER 5

The last rider in Kurt's group was 200 yards ahead. Occasionally Shackleton caught sight of Pablo Rodriguez's gang and he judged that Kurt was gaining on him.

He'd galloped on for another half-mile when gunfire blasted ahead, at first sporadically, but then more determinedly and getting closer. Shackleton wondered whether Pablo had doubled back but on following the riders into a pass he saw that Pablo had decided to make a stand.

His men were scurrying into hiding on one side of the pass while Kurt and his men were dismounting to take up positions on the other side.

They were already trading gunfire and although they'd started with evenly matched numbers the bodies of three men showed that Kurt had made progress in decimating Pablo's group.

By the time Shackleton's group had dismounted, Kurt had accounted for one more.

'How many are we facing?' Shackleton asked when

he scurried into cover beside him.

'Eight tried to escape, and we've already halved that number.' Kurt licked his lips. 'This pass is where Pablo Rodriguez breathes his last.'

Shackleton cast his mind back to the riders he'd seen leaving and he judged that Kurt's total was right, but when he looked at Elwood, he received a shake of the head.

'There was one more than that,' Elwood said.

Kurt dismissed his opinion with a wave of the hand, then settled down to organizing his men to take up the best positions and to lay down gunfire aimed at the opposite side of the pass.

For the next ten minutes they chose their moments to bob up from behind their covering boulders and trade gunfire, but with only starlight available both groups had to pick their targets using merely sound. So neither side threatened the other with the slugs that whined into the rocks around them, frequently landing ten or more yards away.

With everyone getting increasingly exasperated, Barney whispered an idea to Shackleton. Without consulting Kurt, Shackleton agreed.

Two minutes later Barney and Elwood were ready. They slipped out into the pass and crawled forward for twenty yards, then lit the brands they'd made. They hurled them across the pass, getting them as close to Pablo's position as possible, before scurrying back into hiding.

The balls of light hurtled through the night sky. When they'd crashed to the ground in a shower of sparks they bathed the other side of the pass in stark light, leaving their side in relative darkness.

Consequently, the first man to rise and fire got blasted in the chest from two different directions, sending him tumbling forward. Afterwards, the others had the sense to stay down and fire off only the occasional speculative shot, but each time they did, gunfire cannoned around their positions, keeping them pinned down.

'Pablo Rodriguez ain't as ornery as everyone says,' Kurt said happily, glancing at Shackleton. 'Even you managed to take on two of his men.'

Shackleton wondered if he were being insulted, but when Elwood got his attention he dismissed the matter from his thoughts.

'I'm sure I was right,' Elwood said. He pointed out the dead men, then the positions he'd identified as the source of the shooting. 'Nine men hightailed it along Devil's Canyon and I can count only eight here.'

'Then where's the last man?' Shackleton asked, already having concluded who that man was.

'Pablo ain't no yellow-belly,' Barney said, slipping closer. 'So that means he's hiding somewhere to surprise us when he can do the most damage.'

'Then he'd better surprise us soon before we wipe everyone else out.'

Barney and Elwood nodded. Then both men's gazes rose to look up their side of the pass.

Without further comment they slipped away from Kurt's group. In the shadows they followed Elwood to higher ground as he moved towards the position he would have taken if he had wanted to have the most devastating effect.

They were halfway up the pass and had still seen no sign of Pablo, if he were here, when in a burst of recklessness the three men on the opposite side of the pass started firing rapidly. Then they moved to new positions while laying down such a frenetic volley of gunfire that Kurt's group had no choice but to think of self-preservation and keep themselves down.

When the gunfire stopped Kurt and his men rose as one, aiming to pick off any stragglers. At that moment a new volley of shots rang out, but this time they came from this side of the pass.

One man cried out and stumbled forward, followed by a second and third.

'Damn,' Shackleton muttered as he discovered where Pablo had gone to ground in the worst possible way.

The gunfire was coming from behind a tangle of rocks forty yards away. They veered off towards that position and when they'd halved the distance and the shooter swung into view, Shackleton saw that his attention was on the exposed men below as he aimed to inflict as much damage as he could.

Shackleton gestured, directing Elwood and Barney to take a route towards him over higher ground while he took the more direct route. He gave them a few seconds' start then made his way along, putting his faith in the man, presumably Pablo, keeping his attention on the men below.

He'd got to within ten yards of him when he saw Elwood and Barney bearing down on their target from behind. Elwood shook a fist in triumph, signifying he had a clear view of the man.

Shackleton gestured at them to wait for him to get closer. When he'd taken another five paces the man stood again, aiming to blast gunfire at Kurt below. So Shackleton stopped, sighted the man's chest and fired.

Elwood and Barney loosed off shots a moment later. The gunfire slammed into the man's chest and side and made him stand up straight before he keeled over, to lie sprawled over the boulder behind which he'd been hiding.

Shackleton ran, reaching him just as Elwood and Barney leapt down. Shackleton and Elwood kept guns trained on the sprawled man while Barney skirted around the body, then slowly knelt on the boulder.

Barney drew the gun from the body's outstretched and limp hand, the motion dragging a pained grunt from the body. He tossed the gun aside, then he turned the body over.

Shackleton's only sighting of Pablo Rodriguez had been on a wanted poster, but this man was clearly him, and he was still alive.

'Who'd have thought,' Barney said, making to jump down, 'that us three would catch the outlaw Pablo Rodriguez?'

'That ain't our job, Barney,' Elwood said.

'I know, but—'

A gunshot blasted, making Barney cry out, then keel over. He hit the boulder on his side, then slid to the ground.

'Stop that. It's us!' Shackleton shouted, judging that the other side of the pass was too far away to have delivered such an accurate and deadly shot. 'We have Pablo.'

He ventured to look down at Kurt's position and sure enough Kurt was looking up at them with a gun brandished. Then he dismissed Kurt from his thoughts and dropped down to find that Elwood had drawn Barney away from Pablo and was now holding him upright by leaning him against his chest.

The dark, blood-soaked hand that Elwood withdrew showed the wound was serious, and with the wounded Pablo to guard, both men agreed to take no further part in the battle in the pass below.

Ten minutes later Kurt had mopped up Pablo's remaining men, each man fighting until he drew his last breath, but that matter didn't concern Shackleton and Elwood. Barney was dead.

For three years they'd worked together as a team, doing their duty with diligence and skill, then getting into scrapes when they'd unwound between jobs. Always they'd looked out for each other, but somehow Shackleton had never expected this to happen.

By the time Kurt joined them, he was in no mood to join in his gloating.

'How's Barney?' Kurt asked as he kicked the wounded Pablo over.

'Dead,' Shackleton reported, making no attempt to keep the bitterness from his voice.

'I lost four others down there.'

'Only four of your men followed us here!'

Kurt shrugged. 'That's what happens when you take on outlaws like Pablo Rodriguez.'

'Except they died at Pablo's hand. Barney got shot by his own men.'

'That happens too.' Kurt looked down at the sprawling Pablo. 'And it was worth it to get this one.'

'By whose judgement?' Shackleton spluttered.

'By mine.' Kurt drew his gun, aimed down at Pablo's chest, and fired, the shot dragging a pained bleat from Pablo as his body rose, then fell.

'What you doing?' Shackleton snapped, getting to his feet, but Kurt ignored him as he blasted round after round into Pablo's body.

'I'm ensuring that this is one man,' he said as he planted a final bullet in him, 'who doesn't get to have no politician fawning over him.'

The mention of their prime duty shook some of the shock from Shackleton's mind and he turned away from Kurt to tap Elwood's shoulder.

'We're leaving,' he said. 'We've got some live prisoners to guard.'

'Even though I walk through the valley of the shadow of death,' The Preacher intoned, 'I will fear no evil, Psalm twenty-three, verse four.'

'For God's sake stop preaching and help me get this off,' Nathaniel shouted, tearing at the laces to remove his boot.

The prisoners had left them to their fate, but Nathaniel reckoned that if he could knock the dynamite out of the cage that fate might not be the one Turner had wanted.

The stick lay fifteen feet away and beyond his reach, but it was only four feet from the edge of the cage, spluttering through the last inch of fuse.

He slipped his boot off then drew back his arm, but The Preacher grabbed that arm.

'Anyone,' he muttered, his voice shaking with righteous indignation, 'who blasphemes the name of the Lord must be put to death, Leviticus twenty-four, verse sixteen.'

'And you'll join me,' Nathaniel snapped, tearing his hand away. Then he hurled the boot at the stick.

But the act of getting his arm away from The Preacher's grip had veered his aim. The boot flew two feet wide and thudded into the bars.

Nathaniel grunted with irritation and uttered another blasphemy, this time with an added oath, but, as if in answer to his plea, the boot rebounded from the bars, skittered across the base of the cage and nudged the stick.

The force with which it collided was minimal but it was enough to send the stick spinning diagonally across the cage. It came to rest three feet closer to Nathaniel but only a foot from the edge of the cage.

The Preacher provided another appropriate quote predicting that Nathaniel's repeated blasphemies meant he wouldn't enjoy the afterlife, but

Nathaniel didn't plan on finding out whether he was right just yet.

'Be quiet,' he muttered.

'In the beginning,' The Preacher said, 'God created the heavens and the earth.'

Nathaniel removed his other boot. He ignored The Preacher and his ramblings to avoid him causing his aim to veer again as he took careful aim at the stick.

The Preacher continued speaking. 'The earth was formless and empty, darkness was over the surface of the deep.'

The flame spluttered into the stick itself. Only seconds remained. . . .

'The Spirit of God was hovering over the waters.'

Nathaniel drew back his arm then threw the boot.

'And God said . . .' The Preacher said, raising his voice.

The boot flew across the cage and hit the dynamite square on.

'. . . "Let there be light" . . .'

The stick bounded away, hit a bar, bobbed up, looking for a moment as if it would rebound into the cage, but then it sank from view outside.

'But there wasn't light,' Nathaniel shouted, 'Nathaniel one, verse one.'

Then he turned away, curling himself into a ball.

The dynamite exploded, kicking the cage up and sending it tumbling over to land on its side.

The force peppered Nathaniel's back with debris and knocked him into the bars. When the cage came to rest, he and The Preacher lay entangled. His ears were ringing and his limbs were shaking, but he felt more alive than he'd expected to be.

He looked over his shoulder. The dynamite had blown a hole in the base of the cage; its edges were peeling upwards like the petals of a flower.

He breathed a sigh of relief as he appraised the wrecked cage. The dynamite had blown the roof off and left the bars broken and twisted enough to let him slip the manacles away. Then they would be able to get away, provided he could gain The Preacher's co-operation.

'We survived,' he murmured, turning to him and smiling in the hope of finding some common ground. 'Will you help me . . . help us get away?'

But The Preacher's deep-set eyes were staring beyond Nathaniel's shoulder, his hands rising to point.

'And they begged him repeatedly not to order them to go into the abyss, Luke eight, verse thirty-one.'

Nathaniel swung round to see what had shocked The Preacher and saw that the yawning chasm of the canyon was ahead, the force of the blast having thrown them perilously close to the edge.

As he watched the cage tipped, then slid forward a foot. Then, having built up momentum, it inexorably speeded up, rocking back on to its base, then sending them down the slope and into Devil's Canyon.

Within moments all that Nathaniel could see ahead was blackness.

CHAPTER 6

Shackleton and Elwood maintained a steady pace back towards the cage. The horse with Barney's body splayed over the back ensured their mood remained sombre.

Kurt had stayed behind to clear up the aftermath of the gun-battle in the pass, his pleasure in finally getting the second Rodriguez brother in no way diminished by his own losses or his accidental shooting of Barney.

Neither Shackleton nor Elwood gained any such pleasure out of his success.

As they closed on the cage, Elwood veered his horse in to speak to Shackleton for the first time since they'd left the pass.

'I may be wrong,' he said, shrugging as if he were debating whether to mention what was on his mind. 'But back when Barney got shot, I thought I heard gunfire and a loud noise, and it wasn't coming from inside the pass.'

Shackleton hadn't heard anything, but Elwood

had keen ears as well as keen eyes, so he hurried his horse on.

He expected that the fire would mean he would be able to see the cage from some distance away, but they skirted along the edge of Devil's Canyon without seeing it or any lightness ahead, adding to his anxiety.

So it was with some surprise and trepidation that when he at last saw light ahead they were within a hundred yards of the low camp-fire.

Hiram could have let the fire die down but the nervous glances Elwood was casting around continued to make Shackleton uneasy. Accordingly they gave the fire a wide berth, heading for the rill where they'd first encountered Pablo's men.

When they could see the full extent of the area where the boulder had separated the dying fire and the prisoners, they stopped.

All was quiet, with no sign of people or horses or movement.

Worse, the cage wasn't there.

'Whoever flees from the terror,' The Preacher shouted, 'will fall into a pit, Jeremiah forty-eight, verse forty-four.'

Nathaniel gripped hold of the sides of the cage as they slid into the canyon, peering ahead into the blackness beyond. His memory of the canyon in the daylight was of a long slope leading to a distant river. So far the cage had slid down that slope on its base.

But Nathaniel didn't reckon their luck in getting a smooth ride would hold out for much longer. They were speeding up and the cage was rattling so loudly it sounded as if could collapse or tip over at any moment.

With so many bars now broken that event was sure to crush them.

That thought led Nathaniel to look at the bar that secured him to The Preacher. His heart leapt when he saw that it was broken six feet off the base of the cage.

So he raised his arm and the manacles, dragging The Preacher's clutched hands with him, aiming to tip the manacles over the top. He got the chain to within two feet of the top but then The Preacher yanked his arm downwards.

'Remove your scourge from me,' he demanded. 'I am overcome by the blow of your hand, Psalm thirty-nine, verse ten.'

'Talk sense or be quiet,' Nathaniel shouted.

He grabbed The Preacher's hands with both of his own, then twisted him round and dragged him to his feet. He thrust his hands high. The Preacher continued to shout biblical comments at him, but he ignored his protests and with one last lunge he pushed the manacles over the top of the bar.

But as they swung free the cage rocked back and forth, sending them rolling into the bars on the other side and making Nathaniel wish they were still being held securely.

Then the inevitable happened. The sliding cage

hit a rock in its path, which caused it to tip over. Nathaniel felt himself thrown forward to leave the base and he hurtled head first into the darkness.

He waved his arms, frantically searching for something to hold on to but he'd left the cage and he couldn't even see the ground.

All around him was blackness. Wind buffeted his face as he fell, his tumbling motion letting him catch a glimpse of the falling cage above and The Preacher falling with him.

Then the bright sheen of something large and foreboding below came into view, appearing to rush towards him at a rapidly accelerating pace.

After a brief debate Shackleton and Elwood left Barney's horse, then separated to come at the fire and boulder from two different directions. Shackleton chose the side on which the cage had stood.

When he'd moved close enough to the canyon to let the fire slip out of his view he slowed to let his night vision adjust. After pacing his horse forward for another minute he saw the signs of the fight that had taken place here.

Bodies lay beside the boulder and there was a hole in the ground near the edge of the canyon. Deep gouges in the earth and short lengths of bar and torn metal suggested an explosion had taken place; perhaps that had been the noise Elwood had heard.

He dismounted and paced close to the edge to look down into the void. From the scraping indentations near the edge he judged that the cage had tipped over the side.

Whether the prisoners were still inside, he didn't know, but he guessed that one of them hadn't been.

Then he checked on the guards, finding there were four of them, and that they had all been shot repeatedly.

He was aware of Elwood coming closer. After checking the last body, he looked up.

'That accounts for the four guards,' he said, 'but not one of them is Hiram Deeds. I reckon that means some, perhaps all, of the prisoners got away. I wonder what happened, though, to . . .'

Shackleton trailed off when he saw Elwood's grim expression, then he followed him round the boulder. On the other side, bathed in the dying fire's sallow light, was the body of Hiram Deeds, also shot, except the prisoners had given him his own particular end.

The boulder had a sharp overhang and his hanging body dangled from that overhang, swinging in the light breeze as the makeshift gallows provided him with a fate that had awaited Javier Rodriguez and the other prisoners.

'Cut him down,' Shackleton said.

'I guess you can't blame them for doing that to Hiram,' Elwood said as he looked for a way up the boulder.

'In his case, you're right. His double-crossing got him exactly what he deserved.'

By the time Kurt arrived Shackleton had laid out the bodies of the guards in a row and Elwood had picked up the trails of a group of riders who had headed off southwards along the top of Devil's Canyon. The escaped prisoners would have had at most a thirty-minute lead on them, but Shackleton was in no mood for beginning that pursuit until he'd confronted Kurt.

He and Elwood stood beside the boulder, watching Kurt approach. The poor light meant that he went through the same process as they had, of being at first unsure what he could see, followed by a dawning realization of what had happened here.

But Shackleton didn't let Kurt's realization be as slow as his had been.

'Javier Rodriguez has escaped,' he shouted.

Kurt drew his horse to a halt, casting a quick glance across the scene, then looked around as if he might catch sight of Javier hiding close by.

'How do you know that? It looks to me as if the cage got blown up, then fell over the side.'

'It did, but the guards are dead and whoever killed them then made off. We saw several separate prints so even if some prisoners went over the side, most escaped.'

Kurt edged his horse nearer to the edge and peered down into the darkness before approaching Shackleton.

'Someone will have to go down there and check.'

'Someone will, but I'll tell you one thing first. You made some big mistakes—'

'I don't need to hear you questioning my orders no more,' Kurt roared, edging his horse forward to

tower over Shackleton. 'All I need to hear is sugges-
tions on where Javier will go if he's still alive. Then
I'll get him, and this time I ain't leaving it to no judge
to give him a second chance.'

'The only person who gave Javier a second chance
was you.'

Kurt drew his horse back, shaking his head.

'That's the difference between you and me,
Shackleton,' he said. 'I get things done, then worry
about the consequences later. You stand around
whining while prisoners you were supposed to be
guarding get away.'

Shackleton opened his mouth to snap back a
retort, but by then Kurt had already ripped his reins
to the side to turn his horse away and was galloping
off into the night. Shackleton glared at his receding
back until Elwood came over and patted his back.

'That man's a fool,' he said, 'but he was right
about one thing. We can argue about this once we
have Javier Rodriguez back where he belongs.'

Shackleton stayed staring at Kurt until his form
had disappeared into the darkness, then he gave a
begrudging nod. Then they went to their horses.

With their sombre mood returning they collected
Barney's horse. Then they turned their backs on the
direction Kurt had gone and made their way towards
the ridge.

CHAPTER 7

Nathaniel coughed and spluttered, sending water out of his mouth in a seemingly endless torrent. His stomach was so bloated he felt as if he'd swallowed the entire river, and he reckoned the flow would never end.

But when the spasms did, at last, end he found he was lying on his belly on dry ground. He tried to push himself up to a sitting position, but his limbs wouldn't obey him and he stumbled down again to lie on his back.

The sudden motion made his stomach go into spasm again and he coughed up another explosive burst of water. So this time when the spasms ended he lay still, catching his breath. Only when he felt composed enough to move and didn't feel as if he'd vomit again, did he cautiously look around.

It was getting light, the sides of the canyon being visible as brooding slabs of rock that made his neck ache and his head swim before his gaze reached the top.

He lowered his eyes and saw that he was lying beside the river. The Preacher was sitting beside him with his legs drawn up to his chin, looking at the water.

The last thing Nathaniel remembered was falling from the cage and tumbling down into the canyon. The water had been rushing up to meet him, but after that he could recall events in only scrappy, feverish bursts as if he was seeing them by lightning flashes.

The bone-rattling blow of hitting the river, the downwards rush through the cold water, more downward motion, fighting for air, a temporary emergence above water before the river reclaimed him. . . .

Then there were other disjointed memories of Bible quotations and of a strong arm that wrapped itself around his chest and tugged.

He twisted and raised himself on to his elbows so that he could look up at The Preacher. Then he summed up those events in one simple declaration.

'You saved my life,' he said.

Admittedly with them being chained together The Preacher had had no choice but to save his life, assuming, that is, that he had wanted to live. Previously his behaviour had been so bizarre and uninterested in what was happening to him that Nathaniel wouldn't have been surprised if he'd let the river take them both away.

He waited for The Preacher to acknowledge him but that individual continued to watch the water roil by, so Nathaniel stretched himself, finding that, aside from the bruises that announced their presence, he had survived the fall intact.

Feeling stronger now, he rolled himself round to adopt the same posture as The Preacher had, sitting beside him. There, he craned his neck, but he couldn't see the point at which they'd gone over the edge, nor the cage. So he couldn't tell whether they were immediately below that point, or whether they'd drifted downriver.

One thing was certain to him though. If he wanted to remain free for any length of time he couldn't assume that nobody would come down into the canyon to check whether anyone in the cage had survived the fall. They had to get moving.

With the shared manacles around his wrists and ankles that meant he was going nowhere unless he found a way to communicate and agree on a course of action with The Preacher.

He took a deep breath and put on a conversational voice, as if the last few traumatic hours hadn't happened and they were just two men enjoying a pleasant chat beside the river.

'I'm grateful to you for what you did,' he said.

Nathaniel gave him a minute to reply, but The Preacher ignored him.

'Is there anything you want from me in return?'

He waited, but again The Preacher ignored him.

'Do you have a name other than The Preacher?' he tried, without success.

'Then my name is Nathaniel McBain.'

61

Nathaniel was considering what his next comment should be when The Preacher swung his gaze down to consider him, this being the first time Nathaniel could remember him responding to an invitation to speak.

'When Jesus saw Nathaniel approaching,' The Preacher said, 'he said of him, "Here is a true Israelite, in whom there is nothing false". John one, verse forty-seven.'

Nathaniel judged this a good thing, both for the fact that The Preacher had spoken to him and for what he had said.

'I believe there is nothing false about me.' Nathaniel paused, giving The Preacher a chance to speak, but the man didn't take up the offer. 'I'd aimed to live a good life when I got out, but then I got wrongly accused of killing Ramsey Carr and ended up in that cage bound for the gallows.'

This didn't interest The Preacher and the small amount of curiosity in his eyes faded away as he returned to looking at the water.

'Who is this other Nathaniel?' Nathaniel persisted. 'Tell me about him.'

The Preacher didn't take up the opportunity.

So for the next ten minutes Nathaniel talked, hoping he might happen across a comment that would interest The Preacher, stopping from time to time to give him a chance to interject, but the man passed up every opportunity.

Nathaniel spoke of his previous desire to seek a new life and how that hope had been cruelly curtailed. He spoke of his hatred of Turner Jackson for what he'd done, both back at Beaver Ridge and in trying to kill them. He spoke of his desire to ultimately find freedom and to start a new life.

Although he didn't get a response, talking let him put his own thoughts in order and that told him what he had to do next.

He had somehow to clear his name. To do that he had to find Turner Jackson and make him speak the truth. Even if he couldn't get that from him, at the very least he would kill the man who had condemned him to the gallows then tried to blow him up.

That resolve returned him to his original problem: that unless he planned to carry The Preacher to wherever Turner was he needed his help.

He quietened and considered the only comment that had produced a reply so far. He decided that direct questions of a kind that usually worked on other people didn't work on this man. He needed to voice neutral comments that happened to include a biblical context. He had little knowledge of the Bible, so he looked at the river, as The Preacher was doing, and tried to think what might be going through his mind.

'The river is soothing,' he ventured.

'This water,' The Preacher said, speaking for the first time in a while, 'symbolizes baptism that now saves you also, Peter three, verse twenty-one.'

Nathaniel smiled, accepting that his dunking in the water had been a baptism of sorts.

'I suppose I did feel reborn when I came up out of the river.'

63

'And the priests came up out of the river carrying the Ark of the Covenant of the Lord, Joshua four, verse eighteen.'

Nathaniel had no idea what this meant, but he was at least getting responses. He raised his eyes to the lightening sky above the canyon rim.

'A new day dawns,' he said.

The Preacher followed his gaze. 'The path of the righteous is like the first gleam of dawn, shining ever brighter till the full light of day, Proverbs four, verse eighteen.'

'The path of the righteous,' Nathaniel intoned, seizing on the element of that statement that suggested movement, then he cast a glance down-river.

The Preacher followed the direction of Nathaniel's gaze, then rocked himself forward and stood, dragging Nathaniel up to a kneeling position.

'The path of the righteous is level.' The Preacher thrust his hands forward, dragging Nathaniel with him. 'O upright One, you make the way of the right-eous smooth, Isaiah twenty-seven, verse seven.'

Then he set off walking.

Nathaniel hadn't been prepared for him to suddenly accept his suggestion about leaving, so The Preacher stumbled as Nathaniel tried to get his legs moving. Then he got to his feet and fell into stride with The Preacher, hobbling over the stones on his unshod feet.

Within a few paces he matched The Preacher's walking pace and so they strode along beside the river.

Although he didn't want to risk making The Preacher stop now that he was in motion, Nathaniel couldn't help but continue to explore how he might communicate with his odds and for now constant, companion.

'The upright one awaits,' he said, trying to get into the spirit of The Preacher's utterances.

For some reason this comment made The Preacher snort his breath, then stop and swirl round to face Nathaniel, his face darkening.

'The godly have been swept from the land; not one upright man remains.' He grabbed Nathaniel's collar and dragged him up close, spitting his words into his face. 'All men lie in wait to shed blood; each hunts his brother with a net, Micah seven, verse two.'

Then The Preacher released his collar and resumed walking. Nathaniel had no idea what that had meant either, but on reconsidering the words, he decided they hinted at a common purpose, perhaps even of revenge.

That thought made Nathaniel recall one of the few Bible quotations he knew.

'An eye for an eye,' he said, although he presumed he hadn't remembered the exact words, 'a tooth for a tooth.'

'Exodus twenty-one, verse twenty-four,' The Preacher said, nodding as he speeded the pace of his walking.

The women out at the back were wailing again.

Javier Rodriguez thumped the table in irritation,

then swirled round to glare at the post-owner.

'Tell them to be quiet,' he demanded. 'They're being paid enough.'

'They aren't,' the post-owner said, coming out from behind the trading post's counter with two jugs of beer. 'They're my daughters. And they weren't for sale.'

Javier glared at him, wondering if he had shown too much defiance, then leaned back for him to place the jugs on the table. When the post-owner had released the handles, Javier shot out an arm and grabbed his wrist.

'Any more complaints,' he muttered, 'and you won't get to enjoy our custom again.'

The post-owner snorted, clearly debating whether to mention that Javier hadn't paid for any of the vast amount of liquor his group had consumed; then he nodded and returned to the counter.

'What we doing next?' Mitch Cartwright asked.

'I ain't decided,' Javier said, 'but I've got us this far. Trust me. You'll enjoy what comes next.'

Mitch nodded, mollified, but his comment had only gone to make Javier feel even more unsettled.

He didn't know what he wanted to do next.

They'd reached a trading post fifty miles out of Bear Creek and around the same distance from the scene of their escape, so he felt confident that they had thrown off any pursuit.

But previously, when he'd ridden with Pablo, he had always been the one suggesting ideas, which his brother had then usually rejected. Now, this second chance had given him the feeling that he didn't want to live in his brother's shadow any more. With seven ruthless and newly freed condemned men at his side, this was perhaps a chance for him to act on his own.

'We should have seen whether Hiram Deeds had any more dynamite,' Turner Jackson said, grinning. 'Then we could have blown this trading post to hell.'

Javier supped his drink while this comment gathered a round of enthusiastic grunts. Even in the short time he'd spent with these men, he'd gathered that Turner took greater delight at the thought of killing than was normal even amongst men of this type. Blowing things up appeared to give him especial delight.

Over at the counter the post-owner grumbled, making Javier put down his drink and glare at him.

'What did you say?' he demanded.

'I said,' the post-owner said, raising his chin defiantly, 'I thought Pablo Rodriguez was bad, but his brother is even worse.'

Oddly this comment pleased Javier and he leaned back in his chair to look around the post. Several of the men were outside with the post-owner's daughters and those who were inside were riffling through the post's wares with a view to taking what they'd need to remain self-sufficient for as long as possible.

Turner picked up on Javier's more contented mood with surprising speed.

'Is that worse or better?' he asked.

'Depends on which end of a gun you're standing,' Javier said.

Turner nodded, as if his off-hand comment had contained more wisdom than he'd intended.

'So does that mean we're striking out on our own instead of rejoining your brother's gang?'

'We might,' Javier said, leaning forward, intrigued at the way Turner had picked up on his thoughts, almost before he'd finished having them himself.

'I'd have thought,' Mitch said, watching this exchange with bemusement, 'you'd want to continue riding with Pablo after he tried to free you.'

'He only did what you'd expect,' Casey Dawson said, breaking into the conversation for the first time, 'when his brother was behind bars.'

Casey's comment finally let Javier identify his concern.

'I am not Pablo Rodriguez's brother,' he snapped, shaking a fist as he glared at Casey. 'He's *my* brother.'

Mitch and Casey furrowed their brows, murmuring that they didn't understand, but Turner nodded, instantly seeing what he meant.

'You said we'd blaze a trail that'd live in legend for a thousand years,' he said. 'I reckon we will and once we're through, nobody will ever speak of Pablo Rodriguez again, just Javier.'

Javier nodded, then raised the jug to pour himself another glass. Ideas were already forming about all the things Pablo had never wanted to do, which he was now free to explore: train ambushes, the railroad payroll, a new life in Mexico with a woman at his side like Narcissa Maxwell. . . .

But then a particularly loud scream rose up from

outside, making them all look to the door. The door remained closed, but movement caught his eye over by the counter.

Javier started to turn, but Turner had already reacted by raising a gun from beneath the table. Quickly he shot to the side.

Javier turned to see that the post-owner had taken advantage of their being distracted by one of his daughter's screams to drag a rifle up from under the counter. But before he could fire Turner's single shot tore straight between his eyes and sent him tumbling from view, his rifle falling from his grasp.

'Good shooting,' Javier said, standing. He raised his voice. 'Get everybody in and take what we need. We're moving on.'

'We bringing the women?' Turner asked.

'No. Pablo would have, but we have to travel fast.'

Everyone bustled, except for Turner who paced round to stand beside him, adopting a position of being his closest confidant without having been given permission to adopt that role.

'Then I have an idea,' he said, leaning towards Javier and lowering his voice so that only he could hear. 'Something I went back to the cage to do to Hiram Deeds.'

'Go on.'

As the first of the women was pushed back into the post, Turner pointed to a coil of rope looped over a nail on the wall.

'You don't want to be known as Pablo Rodriguez's brother and we don't want to be remembered as another Rodriguez gang.' He went over to the rope and unfurled it, smirking as he looked at the cowering woman. 'It's time to strike fear into everyone's hearts.'

CHAPTER 8

Marshal Kurt McLynn had arrived at the trading post before them.

Shackleton Frost had hoped he wouldn't have to meet Kurt again while he tracked down Javier Rodriguez, but Elwood had led them to a trading post where they'd found him standing outside. He was consulting with several concerned-looking men, and as they approached Shackleton considered how best to conduct what was sure to be a difficult meeting.

But all thoughts of confrontation fled from his thoughts when he saw what Kurt and the group were talking about. Strung up behind the trading post were four dangling bodies, three being young women.

'Just like at Devil's Canyon,' Elwood said, eyeing the women with shock and disgust narrowing his eyes. 'Except these are women, and they're innocent.'

'Javier Rodriguez?' Shackleton asked when he'd

dismounted and joined Kurt.

'Don't know for sure,' Kurt said, turning to him, his expression at least appearing shocked for the first time. 'Nobody here survived, but I'm guessing he gave these women the fate he was due.'

'How long ago and where did he go?'

'It's been around six hours, but I ain't sure where he went. This is a popular post and there's so many trails, there's no working out which one is Javier's.'

'Then let's hope that wherever he goes these four will satisfy his twisted desire to kill.'

Kurt snorted a rueful laugh. 'I ain't confident about that. These men are already talking about the Gallows Gang. It's my guess that as soon as Javier hears that and the fear that comes with it, it'll encourage him to string more people up.'

'Then we have to find him quickly.'

'*We?*'

Shackleton noted that this discovery had driven away some of Kurt's arrogance. His tone was more conciliatory than before, but that didn't stem his own anger.

'You, me, either of us, it don't matter. As long as one of us recaptures Javier Rodriguez before your incompetence lets him kill again.'

Shackleton's comment made Kurt's eyes flare, but aside from snorting his breath, he provided no further sign of his anger. Perhaps, Shackleton wondered, he was now feeling guilty about the results of his failings.

'How did you work out he'd come here?' Kurt asked.

72

'We stayed put and got some sleep.' Shackleton considered Kurt's tired eyes and his stooped posture. 'A man who don't get no sleep ain't much use to anyone. Come daylight we went down into the canyon, but we couldn't find the cage or any sign of survivors.'

'So we're searching for ten men?'

'Eleven. We followed the sole remaining man from Pablo Rodriguez's gang.'

'What man?'

'When we happened across the men lying in wait we knocked out one man, but when we returned he'd gone. Elwood picked up his trail and we followed him. It led here, and with any luck, if we can pick it up again, it'll lead us to Javier.'

'You should have told me about him,' Kurt snapped, regaining some of his former truculence.

'What good would that have done you? It wouldn't have changed anything because you haven't taken any of my advice . . . yet.'

Kurt winced, then looked away while he took deep, calming breaths. When he spoke again his voice was low.

'Don't make me say the words, Shackleton.'

Shackleton snorted a laugh. 'That mean you're admitting you need me?'

'I need able men to help me.'

'Then we ain't much use to you because we won't help you.' Shackleton waited until Kurt opened his mouth to retort, then continued: 'But we will search for Javier Rodriguez and put him behind the bars he

73

should have always remained behind. If you want to help us, you can.'

'Governor Bradbury appointed—'

'He appointed you to deliver Javier Rodriguez to Bear Creek and he appointed me to help you do that,' Shackleton shouted, waving his arms, 'but when your arrogance in ignoring my advice let Javier escape, I reckon all appointments ended.'

Then Shackleton turned away. Elwood stayed to glare at Kurt for a moment longer before joining him.

They had mounted their horses and were turning away from the post when Kurt headed to his horse with his head down. He joined them without comment, leaving the other men to cut down the bodies.

When they left the post they headed away from Bear Creek and, under Elwood's guidance, tracked east and parallel with Devil's Canyon.

Throughout the long afternoon they kept a steady pace each man riding in aggrieved silence with most of the mutual loathing still remaining unspoken. The sun was lowering when Kurt broke the silence.

'Are we following any particular trail, Elwood, or are you guessing?'

'There's a watering hole around five miles on,' Elwood said. 'Javier would have headed for it.'

'And if he didn't?'

'He'll be thirsty and so I'll be even more sure where he went.'

Kurt accepted this information with a curt nod.

'Obliged for the information.'

'And I'll tell you something else that's interesting. We're being followed.'

'Who?' Kurt snapped, turning to Elwood, as did Shackleton, this news also taking him by surprise.

'Ain't sure. It's a lone rider and he's making no attempt to come closer.'

Shackleton resisted the urge to look back, but he put aside that concern soon enough when they approached the watering hole.

Men were milling around it, and he counted eight in total.

They'd been riding through low scrub and the cover was poor enough to mean they would have been seen if the men were being attentive, but the sun was behind them and the afternoon was sultry enough to encourage sloth.

They dismounted. Kurt opened up a telescope to survey the scene. He grunted to himself, then passed it to Shackleton, who saw that the eight men were either resting or roaming around. Their casual postures and attitude suggested they hadn't seen them approach.

Shackleton also grunted when he recognized Javier Rodriguez, then passed the telescope on to Elwood.

'Three against eight,' Shackleton said, 'but that'll work out fine if we can surprise them.'

'We go to ground,' Kurt said, 'split up, and sneak up on them. I'll give the order to attack.'

The matter of who was in charge hadn't been

discussed again so, to avoid an argument, Shackleton quietly glanced at Elwood, who nodded. Then, with a few quick arm movements, Elwood pointed out the best route that would keep them low and hidden and let them get to within yards of the watering hole without being seen.

Kurt agreed to this route, so they collected rope to tie up any prisoners who might survive the forthcoming onslaught. Then they set off, staying together for the first half of the journey, then splitting up for the second 400 yards.

Shackleton walked doubled over, risking a glance upward every fifty paces to orient himself. Each look confirmed that the men were showing no sign of moving out or that they were aware they were being approached.

Fifty yards from the watering hole the scrub petered out, so Shackleton stopped and waited for the signal to attack. He settled down on his belly and picked his targets, the first being Javier Rodriguez, who was standing beside his horse speaking with Turner Jackson.

But then both men swung round to peer towards the sun, their hands coming up to their foreheads as they shielded their eyes. Shackleton winced, his finger tightening on the trigger. But they were looking at a spot that neither Elwood nor Kurt had planned to head for.

Quickly, the other men stopped whatever they were doing and joined Javier in looking. Then hoofbeats pounded, approaching fast.

'Our follower,' Shackleton murmured to himself. He turned his gaze away from Javier, looking to see who was coming.

The hoofbeats stopped. A horse whinnied. Then, from the corner of his eye, Shackleton saw Javier drop to his knees, the other men did the same, then scrambled into hiding.

'Don't be a fool!' Kurt shouted, his voice coming from fifty yards to Shackleton's right.

With the element of surprise gone, Javier and his men started firing blind while scrambling for their horses.

Shackleton fired off a couple of shots that splayed wide, then he slipped back into the scrub and ran towards where he'd heard the sound of Kurt's voice.

He'd covered half the distance when the horse and rider came into view. He was shocked to see that their follower was a woman. Kurt had looped a hand around the harness and she was trying to tear herself loose.

Gunfire erupted from over by the watering hole, making Kurt flinch away; this let the woman shake herself free. Her horse reared before she got it under control. Then she spurred it to head on to the hole.

Shackleton put Javier from his mind and uncoiled the rope he'd brought along. He played it out, swung a loop twice around his head, then threw it. The woman was building up to a trot when the rope landed with unerring accuracy over the horse's head.

Shackleton planted his feet wide, but the trotting horse still dragged him on, heading straight for the

77

open area. Half-running, half-stumbling while trying to dig in his heels Shackleton staggered on, but then Elwood joined him and a second lasso came down on the horse's head.

With the two men pulling back from either side of her, they drew the horse to a halt. Only then did Shackleton look to the watering hole, but it was to see a cloud of dust as Javier and his men made the best use of this distraction to make good their escape.

Kurt went sprinting after them but, from the redness of his face, Shackleton judged it was more out of anger than from a feeling that he would achieve anything. And it would have to be on his own as Shackleton didn't like the thought of leaving the woman and risking her making another foolish dash towards the escaped prisoners.

Slowly, Shackleton and Elwood drew in the rope until they stood beside the horse. The woman struggled and tried to move the horse on in every direction. Then eventually she relented, lowered her head and sobbed.

Shackleton motioned for Elwood to keep a firm grip of his rope. Then he released his own rope and helped the woman down. But then she shook him off, sat on the ground, and bawled.

Nothing Shackleton could say could stem the flow of tears that marred her otherwise pretty, oval face, so he consulted with Elwood, who for once found himself with a problem for which he didn't have an answer. So they waited.

Ten minutes later the woman stopped snivelling, and five minutes after that a glowering Kurt returned, having accepted that Javier had got away, for now.

'She all right?' he asked.

'I think she will be, but what was she doing?'

'We want Javier because that's our job,' Kurt said, kneeling down beside her. 'But Narcissa Maxwell wants him for revenge.'

At the mention of her name, Narcissa looked up. Despite her distress her voice was reasonably composed.

'You had no right to stop me. You know what the Rodriguez gang did to me.'

'I've heard the stories. That's why Mayor Maxwell . . . your father called in a US marshal to bring them to justice.'

'And yet Javier is now free.'

'Not for long.' Kurt offered the kindest smile Shackleton had ever seen him deliver, then turned to him. 'Two of us should follow Javier. I'd suggest Elwood should escort her back to Bear Creek, or at least to someone who can take care of her.'

'I can take care of myself,' the woman murmured sulkily before Shackleton could reply. 'And besides, if you're not letting me deal with Javier on my own, you all have to go back to Bear Creek.'

'Why?'

'The news is out about Javier escaping. So my father wants to talk to you.'

'We can't waste time talking to him,' Kurt said, for

79

once speaking for Shackleton too. 'We're only minutes behind Javier.'

'Father was adamant, as is Governor Bradbury.'

'And who are they to tell me what to do?' Kurt muttered.

Shackleton couldn't help but utter a rueful laugh.

'And who are you, Kurt,' he said, 'to question anyone's commands?'

CHAPTER 9

'May the groans of the prisoners come before you,' The Preacher said. 'By the strength of your arm preserve those condemned to die, Psalm seventy-nine, verse eleven.'

The smith looked at Nathaniel, gulping, and Nathaniel offered him a smile.

'I reckon he's asking you to be careful with that hammer,' he said.

The smith nodded, then raised the hammer high.

The Preacher and Nathaniel had walked for most of the day and had emerged from Devil's Canyon as the sun had disappeared from view. The small settlement of Wilson's Crossing was at the mouth of the canyon and had saved them from having to spend a second night outside.

Luckily, the collection of houses included a stables and an adjoining smithy.

The arrival of two shackled men had raised the kind of consternation Nathaniel had expected, and the smith had been all set to slam the door on them and hurry off, presumably to fetch a gun.

Then he'd seen The Preacher and the sight had made him fall to his knees.

The smith was six inches taller than even the rangy preacher was and had arms that were as thick as Nathaniel's legs, but that didn't stop him begging them to leave him alone. Nathaniel had promised him they would, but only after he'd separated them; the plea had resulted in the smith dragging the manacled pair to an anvil.

Five solid blows separated the manacles around their ankles and two more dealt with their wrists. Then the smith removed the remaining rings from around The Preacher's limbs.

The moment the last ring fell, The Preacher stood and paced to the door. The smith watched him walk away murmuring to himself. Only when he'd passed through the door did the smith turn to Nathaniel.

'Where's he going? What's he doing? I have a wife and children. Will—?'

'I'm sure he just wants to leave here and never return. As do I.' Nathaniel cast a significant glance at his own remaining bands of iron. The smith hastily removed them.

'We don't want no trouble,' the smith said, backing away as Nathaniel stretched his arms and legs, enjoying the lightness of his limbs and the ease with which he could move them for the first time in a while.

'Neither do we, and this ain't what it seems so don't speak of this to anyone. We just want to leave.'

Nathaniel knew of the difficulty of getting metal so he gestured at the fallen ironwork. 'Keep that in payment for your help.'

'Obliged.'

Nathaniel turned to the door, but with the weight gone from his limbs, another insistent urge rippled through his stomach and he turned back.

'And in return, we wouldn't mind some food. We haven't eaten in a while.'

'And then you'll take that man away?'

Nathaniel nodded, although he'd hardly finished the gesture before the smith dashed outside.

Within a minute the smith returned, casting wide-eyed, scared looks to the side, presumably at The Preacher, then he thrust a bundle at Nathaniel.

Nathaniel took the bundle and thanked him, then thanked him again when a glance inside revealed that he'd been more than generous with bread, cheese, strips of beef.

When he was outside he turned back to face the scared smith.

'What has The Preacher done to make you that worried?' he asked.

The smith gulped. 'You mean you don't know and you're his partner?'

'I ain't exactly his—' Nathaniel didn't get to complete his comment as the smith then slammed the door. Nathaniel knocked, then pushed open the door. 'Why are you so worried?'

He didn't get an answer, but he did get something even more welcome when the smith hurled his boots at him, shouting at him to just get away.

Nathaniel looked at the closed door, wondering if he should take the smith's fear seriously. He now had food, was free to walk alone and more comfortably than before, and he could set out to track down Turner without being accompanied by his babbling, and presumably dangerous, companion.

But when he turned he found that The Preacher was waiting for him.

He stood beside the river looking away from Devil's Canyon and the route they'd previously been taking. So, seeing that he had no choice for now, Nathaniel sat down to slip the smith's boots on, then joined The Preacher.

That night they settled down in a dry wash overlooking Wilson's Crossing. Nathaniel reckoned he could gather enough dry wood for a fire, but he assumed that a pursuit could be getting closer by now, so he decided not to risk it.

He opened up their food bundle and laid it out, letting The Preacher select what he wanted to eat first.

To his surprise The Preacher reacted to the food in a way that was the nearest to normal behaviour he'd seen. He divided up the bread and cheese into six segments, then allocated the meat strips between each segment.

'Taking the five loaves and the two fish and looking up to heaven,' he said as he worked, 'he gave thanks and broke them, Luke nine, verse sixteen.'

Then he tore the cloth into two and bound up

four of those segments into small packages, leaving two.

When he took one of those segments, Nathaniel saw that he'd worked out a sensible amount to eat and had ensured they had food for the next few days.

'Do you want to bless the food?' Nathaniel asked as he took his share.

'A generous man will himself be blessed, for he shares his food with the poor, Proverbs twenty-two, verse nine.'

'I know. That smith was a generous man.' Nathaniel laughed. 'It's a pity we didn't ask him for more.'

The Preacher didn't respond to this and they ate their food in silence.

Later Nathaniel made himself comfortable on the soft earth. With a full belly for the first time in days, he quickly went to sleep.

But it wasn't a restful sleep.

Despite Nathaniel's having appeared to have reached some sort of understanding with The Preacher, the smith's shock at the mere sight of the man had troubled him.

Every time he awoke he looked over towards The Preacher, who had found a position to sleep in that let him sit upright. He was mumbling to himself, either in sleep or while awake.

As the night wore on The Preacher and his constant biblical murmuring invaded Nathaniel's dreams so vividly that he wasn't sure whether he was dreaming or awake.

Repeatedly the fear on the smith's face, along with that of the prisoners, came back to him and echoed in his mind, as did Mitch Cartwright's taunt about The Preacher eating him.

Later Nathaniel found himself trapped in a nightmare that seemed real, where The Preacher loomed over him, his gaunt face closing in. The Preacher opened his mouth far wider than he should have been able to. A long serpent-like tongue emerged and licked his face, rasping the skin away.

'It's a dream,' Nathaniel shouted, trying to wake himself, but the tongue kept rasping and The Preacher's face came closer and closer and. . . .

With a scream on his lips, either in his dream or in the waking world, Nathaniel sat upright, shaking himself awake and seeing that dawn had come.

Then a huge face pushed itself towards him, a tongue emerging to lick his face, and he screamed again. He rolled and came to his feet ready to fight back and found with some embarrassment that what he'd taken for The Preacher's face was in fact a horse's.

He looked up to see that The Preacher was riding that horse and that he'd brought along a second mount.

Still shaking, Nathaniel stood up and made his way over to the second horse. He saw the loaded saddle-bags, and when he looked at The Preacher he saw that he had a gun at his hip.

'Where did you. . . ?' Nathaniel trailed off, remembering the comment he'd made last night about how it was a pity they hadn't asked the generous smith for more.

Nathaniel mounted up and from his higher position he looked towards the river and Wilson's Crossing.

'This water,' The Preacher said, 'symbolizes baptism that now saves you also, Peter three, verse twenty-one.'

Nathaniel had heard this quote after The Preacher had saved his life, so he took this as a good sign.

But he still murmured a silent prayer that the smith and his family had provided these goods willingly. Then he joined The Preacher in heading off, taking a direction that was broadly eastwards.

'Where are we going?' he asked.

'His own actions were evil and his brother's were righteous,' The Preacher said, 'John three, verse twelve.'

Nathaniel didn't reckon that that answered his question, but they were heading away from Devil's Canyon and so in the same direction as he assumed Javier Rodriguez, Turner Jackson and the rest had gone. So that direction was good enough for him, and it felt even better when he explored the saddlebags and found that The Preacher had obtained a gun for him too.

With the gun at his hip, Nathaniel rode tall in the saddle.

'An eye for an eye,' he said.

'A tooth for a tooth,' The Preacher agreed.

'Exodus twenty-one, verse twenty-four,' Nathaniel said, surprising himself with his memory; then he glanced over at The Preacher.

He couldn't be sure, but he thought he detected a smile.

CHAPTER 10

'And the worst thing about this is,' Mayor Maxwell said, as he thought of yet another angle with which to berate Kurt and Shackleton. 'I have invited the state governor to come to our very town next week to see me deal with Javier Rodriguez. He said that we were a shining beacon of hope for small towns everywhere. What can I tell him now? That he can't come because our beacon has been ground into the dirt by the two men I trusted the most?'

'We—' Kurt began, but Maxwell hadn't finished.

'And don't tell me that I should stop our town's proud day just because you two are so incompetent as to let ten of the worst outlaws this county's ever known escape.'

Neither Shackleton nor Kurt would have presumed to tell Maxwell anything, as they appeared to stand no hope of getting a word in to explain themselves.

Previously Shackleton had been in a quandary as to what he should say. If they'd met Maxwell and the governor of Beaver Ridge jail immediately after Kurt had shot Barney in the back, he'd have had no problem telling them what he thought about him.

But faced with such a tirade he reckoned presenting a united, albeit silent, front was his best and probably only option.

'For me,' Governor Bradbury said, when Mayor Maxwell paused to take a drink of water, 'the worst thing is I recommended you two and then defended you when the mayor questioned whether we had enough men for the job. He'd have given me fifty but I said a small team of the lawman who brought in Javier Rodriguez and the man who's never lost a prisoner would get the job done. How do you think that makes me look?'

Governor Bradbury waited, but neither man replied, judging that, like Mayor Maxwell, he didn't want an answer, and that he was saying whatever he had to say to direct the mayor's anger away from himself.

'It makes you look,' Mayor Maxwell said, 'as bad as I do. So I sure as hell ain't cancelling the governor's visit and I sure as hell will send Javier Rodriguez to the gallows before his very eyes next week.'

Silence reigned for several seconds and taking it that this time they did want an answer, Kurt spoke up.

'After we eliminated Pablo Rodriguez with our small force, taking serious losses in the process, we picked up on Javier's trail. Your dragging us away from that pursuit means it'll have gone cold, but we will recapture him and the rest of the escaped prisoners long before the governor's visit.'

'See that you do,' Governor Bradbury snapped, his eyes flaring after Kurt had offered a veiled criticism of his own actions. 'You have seven days or neither of you will ever work for me again.'

'And I have enough connections,' Maxwell said, 'to ensure neither of you will ever work for anybody ever again.'

He glared at each man in turn to check that they understood he had the political power to carry through with his threat, leaving Governor Bradbury to point at the door.

'So why are you standing around here talking?' he demanded. 'You've got a prisoner to get back behind bars where he belongs!'

Kurt nodded and started to turn away, but Maxwell raised a hand, halting him.

'And,' he said, his tone low, 'I am grateful that you brought Narcissa back safely. After what the Rodriguez brothers did to her, I can't blame her for being hot-headed enough to seek her own revenge.'

Kurt nodded, then joined Shackleton in leaving. Once they were outside the mayor's office, Shackleton heard a new argument starting up inside, presumably one in which each man made it clear to the other that the escape wasn't *his* fault. They didn't stay to hear its conclusion.

'All right, Shackleton,' Kurt said as they headed down the boardwalk. 'You don't like me and my methods and I ain't particularly taken with the way you question my every move, so do we split up or do we work together?'

Shackleton gave the matter serious thought before he replied.

'We work together as a team. If we disagree, the majority decides.'

'So be it.' Kurt halted and waited for Elwood, who pushed himself away from the hitching rail where he'd been talking with another man and made his way over to them. 'What's your suggestion?'

'We go back to the watering hole. If we make good time, we should get there by early afternoon.'

'After a day, the trail will be too cold. We need to stop thinking like trackers and think like lawmen. There was something plain odd about Narcissa Maxwell heading off after Javier on her own. I reckon we should question her when she's calmed down.'

Shackleton didn't know the history of what had happened to her at the hands of the Rodriguez brothers, but he could guess, so he turned to Elwood to make the casting vote.

'I've got my own suggestion,' he said. 'While Maxwell was bursting your eardrums I asked around. There's been a killing at Wilson's Crossing.'

Shackleton winced. 'Javier Rodriguez?'

'No,' Elwood said. 'It's worse. It's The Preacher.'

'So,' Mitch Cartwright said, 'we'll ambush a train only because Pablo never wanted to?'

'Yeah,' Turner Jackson said before Javier could reply. 'And I say it's a good idea.'

'So do I, but . . .' Mitch looked around the saloon as he gathered his thoughts. 'But I reckon we can do so much more if we join back up with Pablo.'

'We could do so much less,' Javier said, entering into this argument for the first time. 'My brother has no ambition, no vision. And that's why his greatest achievement will always be that he is my brother.'

Mitch wisely gave up on the argument and wandered off down the bar to join Casey.

Yesterday, everyone had worked off their frustrations at the trading post. So now they'd holed up at Baxter's Point, a forgotten two-bit fleapit of a town that clung to the side of a ridge like a particularly irritating boil. Nobody would ever stop in a place like this, which is precisely why he and Pablo had often stopped here.

The former prisoners who had now become his to command were drinking in pensive mood as they awaited his decision as to what they did next.

In the short time they'd been free Mitch and Turner had become Javier's closest advisers, with Turner advocating that they strike out on their own and better Pablo's exploits. Mitch advocated rejoining Pablo.

Javier had favoured Turner so far, but he enjoyed hearing Mitch present an alternative point of view, and he hadn't put his own suspicions about Turner from his mind. It had been rumoured he'd had a part with Nathaniel McBain in ensuring that the prison breakout had failed, whereas Mitch had been the ringleader in organizing that breakout.

There was no way of knowing now whether those rumours were true, but he had resolved to keep both men close, carefully weigh up their actions, then make a judgement on whom he could trust the more later.

On this current matter, he had already decided to side with Turner. They would hold up a train, something Pablo had always been loath to do. Turner understood why he had to do it, but the others didn't. He was musing on why that was the case when Turner sidled along the bar to him.

'Mitch is getting to be trouble,' he said from the corner of his mouth.

Javier snorted. He had expected him to make a comment like that.

'It's nothing I can't deal with. I'm not like Pablo. I listen to what my men have to say.'

'Then listen to this. The railroad is a fine start, but for a man with ambition, we have to think even bigger than that, and we can start with Bear Creek's bank.'

Javier was minded to agree and press him for more details when he heard a rider approaching outside. He glanced at the bartender who winked, a simple signal to say the newcomer had already been sized up and the message passed inside that he represented no problem to anyone here.

But Javier hadn't expected that Jim Parker would enter. He was trail-dirty and his features were thunderous as he looked around the saloon. His mood didn't lighten as he made his way over to Javier.

Jim had ridden with Pablo since the beginning and if Pablo were to pick anyone to pass a message on to him it would be Jim.

'What's my brother got to say for himself?' he said.

'He ain't saying nothing no more,' Jim said. 'That lawman Marshal Kurt McLynn killed him.'

'Him again,' Javier spat. Around the saloon everyone looked at him with a mixture of embarrassment and perhaps even shame in their eyes. After he'd spent most of the last day saying how he planned to move on without his brother, he couldn't blame anyone.

'Yeah,' Jim said, 'and he got every last one of us.'

Javier raised an eyebrow, regaining some of his composure.

'Yet you survived.'

'Sure did. Someone had to let you know what happened.'

'And how did it happen?'

'That lawman ambushed us,' Jim said, then went on to describe the events in Devil's Canyon of which he'd seen only the aftermath.

Javier didn't pay those details much attention as he put his own thoughts about this revelation in order. The tale only piqued his interest when Jim moved on to describe what he'd found out about them since the ambush.

'Say that again,' he said.

'They've got a name for you,' Jim said as Turner punched the air. 'You ain't been free for long, but already you're known as the Gallows Gang.'

Javier patted Turner's back. 'We kind of figured that'd happen.'

'But that don't matter none. The Pablo Rodriguez gang is still in force. You ready to ride now and make that lawman regret ever hearing of us?'

'No. Pablo died because he was a clumsy fool. Nobody will remember him.'

Jim's mouth opened wide in shock.

'You have to,' he murmured, backing away a pace. 'Kurt killed your brother.'

'I don't *have* to do nothing no more.'

Jim shot a glance down the bar at Turner, who grunted that he agreed with Javier. Then he looked around the rest of the saloon. He received nothing but blank expressions.

'You're all yellow-bellied critters,' Jim muttered, his face reddening.

Then he threw his hand to his holster, but he didn't get to reach it as Javier's low shot to the guts bent him double. A slug from Turner a moment later sent him crashing into the bar where he clung on for a moment before sliding down it to lie sprawled on the floor.

'Anyone else got a problem with me not going after the lawman?' Javier said, pacing up to the body.

Nobody replied, but he noticed that neither did anyone meet his eye. Turner was the first to react.

'Swift, Casey,' he said, gesturing, 'check he wasn't being followed.'

Javier glanced at Turner and nodded, acknowledging that was a wise precaution, then he kicked over Jim's body to turn him on to his back. He looked into his lifeless eyes, noting that, aside from himself, he was the last tie with the Pablo Rodriguez gang.

'The Gallows Gang,' he said, rolling his tongue around the words and relishing their sound.

'Why Baxter's Point?' Nathaniel asked, looking past the town sign to appraise the unpromising-looking collection of buildings ahead.

The Preacher didn't respond other than to stop and stare silently ahead.

From somewhere, perhaps the saloon, gunfire sounded and this made him draw his horse to the side, then pace into the scrub until he disappeared from sight. Nathaniel heard him dismount and with a last bemused look towards town he followed him.

'This place sure is a dead-end town,' he said when he joined him, but The Preacher declined the opportunity to provide a sage and cryptic biblical quotation.

Nathaniel had let The Preacher lead him here and even for someone whose every utterance was enigmatic, his explanations had been particularly obscure.

But quotations that referred to brothers had been common, so Nathaniel had deduced that The Preacher was on the trail of one of the Rodriguez brothers and for now that was good enough for him.

How he was following that trail Nathaniel didn't know and he'd resigned himself to not getting any straight answers. But any residual scepticism slipped away when he saw two men head out of the saloon, then make their way towards them.

They were Swift Tate and Casey Dawson, two men whom he'd last seen running away after Turner Jackson had rolled the dynamite into the cage.

He lost his last reservations about what The Preacher's motivations were when the man slowly removed his gun from its holster, dropped to his knees, and crawled through the scrub towards the town sign.

Nathaniel followed, joining him when he stopped a few yards from open ground and ten yards from the sign, at a point where the two men would pass within a few yards of them.

They waited in silence while the two men carried on until they reached the sign, where they scanned the land ahead of them, then back towards the saloon.

'Jim Parker ain't no idiot,' Casey said. 'He won't have been followed.'

'I know that,' Swift said, 'but Turner reckons that by ordering us around he wins favour with Javier.'

'I figured that too.' Casey leaned on the sign and felt in his pocket for a smoke. 'I don't trust that man.'

'Me neither. I reckon Mitch is talking more sense.'

'Like he always does.' Casey glanced around, taking in the fading light. 'I reckon we should stay here for another ten minutes, then go back in and report it's all clear.'

Swift agreed with this plan, and the two men leaned back against the sign, smoking.

Nathaniel watched them until he was sure they

were relaxed and off-guard. Then he glanced at The Preacher, wondering how they could work out between them what they should do now, but The Preacher's next pronouncement left him in no doubt as to what he planned to do.

'For the day of vengeance was in my heart,' The Preacher murmured, 'and the year of my redemption has come, Isaiah sixty-three, verse four.'

Then The Preacher rose from the scrub like a towering, vengeful angel of death, his gun swinging up to aim at the men.

His movement rustled the undergrowth and made the men twist nervously round to face him, their hands twitching for their guns, but before they reached them The Preacher's gun roared, taking Swift high in the chest and spinning him away.

Casey spat out a mouthful of smoke as he reached for his own gun, but Nathaniel blasted a single shot into his stomach, making him stagger back a pace. The Preacher finished him with a slug to the centre of his forehead.

Then The Preacher lowered himself back into the scrub.

Nathaniel had hoped that they might take one of the men alive so that they could find out everything they could about the other escaped prisoners. So he moved to head out of the scrub and see if either of them still lived, but The Preacher shot out a hand and grabbed his arm, halting him.

'Bring into the ark two of all living creatures, Genesis six, verse nineteen.'

'Do you mean we should let them come out in twos and we'll pick 'em off?'

The Preacher didn't acknowledge whether he had understood him correctly, but Nathaniel took his lack of response to mean he had.

So they waited.

Within a minute the gunfire made one man edge outside the saloon, then a second. They looked towards the town sign and the bodies lying beside it, then conferred and slipped back into the saloon.

Presently Turner Jackson emerged with Javier Rodriguez at his side. This sight made Nathaniel mutter under his breath.

He had imagined that his quest to find Turner might take months, but The Preacher had led him straight to him, another consideration that made him grateful to have his odd companion at his side.

Javier and Turner were around 200 yards away, but Nathaniel could see that Javier was asking Turner for advice.

Turner's arm-waving suggested he was being free with his comments. Putting this observation together with Casey and Swift's overheard conversation, Nathaniel decided that Turner had already wormed himself into Javier's confidence.

'Be careful, Javier,' Nathaniel murmured to himself. 'That snake will turn on you like he did on me and all the others.'

'You snakes,' The Preacher said, 'you brood of vipers. How will you escape being condemned to hell? Luke three, verse seven.'

'They won't,' Nathaniel said. 'But I prefer to say it's two down, six to go, and when they get a little bit closer it'll be—'

Cold steel stabbed into the back of his neck, silencing him.

He risked glancing back to see that three men he remembered as having guarded the cage had sneaked up on them. The man with a gun on The Preacher wore a star.

The Preacher dropped his gun, as did Nathaniel, making the lawman smile.

'You got it wrong, Nathaniel McBain,' he said. 'It's two more down, six to go.'

CHAPTER 11

'If you want to get the Gallows Gang,' Nathaniel said, raising his arms, 'you'll need our help.'

'We had all the help we needed from you when we followed you here,' Kurt said, as Javier and Turner returned to the saloon.

Shackleton saw Kurt's muscles grow tense. His gun rose a fraction.

'You'd better not be planning on dealing with these men like you did with Pablo Rodriguez,' he said.

Kurt lowered his gun slightly from its steady aim at The Preacher's head.

'What you planning to do about it if I do?'

'I'll stop you.'

'Don't be a fool. You saw what they did back at Wilson's Crossing. We've got at least six men to take on in the saloon. We can't look after these two as well.'

'You mean that *you* can't. Elwood and me – and Barney – spent years looking after prisoners and we never mistreated one, or lost one.'

Kurt sneered and raised his gun, but Shackleton swung his own gun away from its steady aim at Nathaniel to turn it on Kurt. Elwood also stepped forward and turned his gun on Kurt.

'You wouldn't shoot a lawman,' Kurt said, looking at each man in turn.

'Don't find out the hard way,' Shackleton said in a low and determined tone. 'Lower your gun.'

Nathaniel turned his head, his eyes reflecting his surprise that they were prepared to shoot each other over them, although The Preacher kept his gaze set forward.

Kurt looked at the two captured men. Then, with a shake of his head, he lowered his gun.

'These men are all yours to look after.'

'That's fine with us,' Shackleton said.

Kurt pointed at Shackleton. 'But if you ever turn a gun on me again, you'd better be prepared to pull that trigger because I sure as hell will blast you away.'

Shackleton nodded, then looked towards the saloon.

'And now if we've settled that matter, we should get the men we came for.'

Kurt grunted that he agreed with that, so Elwood stepped forward to pull The Preacher to his feet. Shackleton did the same to Nathaniel.

'You two won't give us no trouble, will you?' Elwood said.

The Preacher ignored him, but Nathaniel looked over his shoulder at Shackleton.

'We won't, but I didn't deserve to be in that cage heading for the gallows. Turner Jackson is the only man who knows that to be the case and he's in the saloon. Let me help you and I'll get him to speak the truth.'

Elwood exchanged an amused glance with Shackleton. After three years delivering prisoners to Beaver Ridge jail they had heard every kind of protestation of innocence imaginable.

'Yeah, yeah, save it for the judge,' Shackleton said, pushing Nathaniel forward.

'But—'

'I said be quiet! Like Kurt said we saw the bodies you left behind in Wilson's Crossing. You'd better save your breath to explain that one away.'

This comment made Nathaniel bow his head in shame, now knowing that the smith had not given the goods willingly.

Given more time Shackleton would have tied the prisoners up, but he couldn't now that the men inside the saloon had been alerted to the fact that something was wrong and after Kurt had wasted time arguing. So he and Elwood stayed back letting Kurt pace into town at the front.

Kurt took a path close to the few buildings and walked with the steady confidence of someone who had visited this town before and knew this to be a safe route. With his head held high and his gun drawn and held low he walked straight towards the saloon.

Elwood caught Shackleton's eye with a look that said he couldn't believe how reckless he was being with Javier Rodriguez being inside, but when Kurt approached the saloon's only window he veered to the side.

He pressed himself to the wall, listening, then edged round the side of the saloon to the back.

Although Kurt hadn't given any instructions Shackleton and Elwood followed. When they reached the back they got all the explanations they needed for his actions.

'Like I thought,' he said, peering round the back corner. 'While you were busy questioning my orders, those damn varmints have hightailed it out of here.'

Shackleton ignored the misplaced rebuke and joined Kurt in looking at the back, seeing that the ground fell away sharply behind the saloon, with a trail zigzagging its way down into the gathering gloom. A door at the back of the saloon was open.

When Shackleton recalled the scene at the front of the saloon he remembered seeing only a few horses: not enough for the whole Gallows Gang. Three steeds were mooching around at the back, presumably owned by the shot men.

'The horses?' he asked.

Kurt sighed. 'Yeah. I'd better see who's left inside. I might be able to shake something out of them.'

Kurt headed to the door and moved to walk in, but then flinched back a pace and gestured for Shackleton to join him.

Shackleton glanced inside and saw that a man was dangling from a gibbet beside the door, although gunshot wounds marred his chest.

'I recognize him,' he said. 'He's the man we followed back in Devil's Canyon.'

'So they're turning on each other now,' Kurt said. 'But is that a good sign or a bad one?'

'Take it all,' Javier shouted to the remaining members of the Gallows gang. 'Then we ride.'

Three of the men, Chester, William, and Aaron whooped with delight then made their way down the aisle, leaving Mitch and Turner to stay with Javier and cover the frightened passengers.

'Going well, ain't it?' Turner asked, looking at Mitch.

Mitch shrugged. 'I still reckon trains provide slim pickings unless you know there's some mighty interesting cargo on board.'

'Interesting cargo means heavily guarded trains. This is easy money before we move on to raiding Bear Creek's bank.'

Javier hadn't agreed to Turner's plan yet, but he let the argument bounce back and forth between them, as it had done since he'd decided to raid the train bound for Bear Creek.

This was something that Pablo too had always said wasn't worth the effort. So it felt right that this should be his first raid since the news had got out about the demise of the Pablo Rodriguez gang and the rise of the new, more ruthless Gallows Gang.

It took his men ten minutes to work their way around the passengers and the reputation that preceded them meant everyone handed over their

106

money and valuables without complaint or any sign of fighting back. When they'd been through the car, Javier was about to order his men to move out, but Turner raised a hand.

'Perhaps Mitch was right,' he said, this comment taking Mitch aback. 'This raid will only be worth the effort if there's some interesting cargo here. We should check out the other cars.'

'I guess we could,' Mitch said.

They'd already seen that there were only a few unpromising-looking crates and boxes stored on the train, but Javier judged that if checking helped to get Mitch and Turner to agree on something, it'd be worth the delay.

'Do it,' Javier said, 'but do it quickly.'

Mitch and Turner hurried off while the other surviving members of the Gallows Gang, Chester, William, and Aaron slipped past him and jumped down from the train.

Javier slipped into the doorway to the car and eyed the frightened passengers, wondering if they had enough time to hang someone and so add to their ruthless reputation.

But then a gunshot blasted nearby, coming from the direction Mitch and Turner had gone, closely followed by a second shot.

Javier issued a quick order that none of the passengers should move if they wanted to live, then hurried off through the deserted cars.

He reached the end one, where he found the same collection of unpromising crates and boxes that he remembered, except that now Mitch was lying sprawled over one crate, a gunshot wound marring his back. A prone and dead engineer provided the story of what had happened, but Javier still demanded an explanation.

'He was lying in wait,' Turner said, pointing at the engineer. 'He came up from behind a box without warning and shot Mitch in the back.'

'String him up quickly as a warning that this is what happens to anyone who takes on the Gallows Gang. Then we ride before anything else goes wrong here.'

'We did get something though,' Turner said, smirking as he patted the crate over which Mitch lay. 'We got ourselves some dynamite – ideal for a bank raid.'

Javier told Turner to bring the crate. Then they strung up the dead engineer and made their hurried departure.

It was only when they'd put several miles between them and the raided train that it occurred to Javier that he hadn't seen a gun in the engineer's hand.

CHAPTER 12

'What did he say?' Shackleton asked as Kurt rode up on to the mound.

From his sitting position Nathaniel watched Kurt dismount and join Shackleton in looking down at the group of men, who were standing beside the railroad and listening intently as Mayor Maxwell gave them his orders.

He crossed his fingers behind his back in hope that these wouldn't prove to be his last moments of relative freedom.

'He said plenty,' Kurt said, 'and none of it was cheering. Despite Javier still being on the loose, the governor is still coming.'

'Hence all those men?'

'Yup. Mayor Maxwell had said he had fifty men at his disposal to find Javier. It seems he's decided to use them, except if they don't find him, it'll be us that'll take the blame.'

Elwood looked up from where he was guarding Nathaniel and The Preacher.

'Fifty men make a lot of noise,' he said. 'If that don't make Javier go to ground, nothing will.'

'I know, but only twenty will be out looking for him. He's putting ten on the next train to make sure the governor gets here safely. Another ten will be guarding the next railroad payroll, and another ten are out searching for Narcissa. She went looking for Javier again.'

'Then this time,' Elwood said, 'I hope she has more luck than we're having.'

Kurt nodded, then pointed at their prisoners.

'Either way, we can get some use out of these two. Mayor Maxwell has one body to show the governor. I've told him where he can find three more, but I reckon he'd enjoy having two live ones he can string up in front of the governor.'

'I'm surprised,' Shackleton said, 'you didn't mention them when you were down there.'

'Like you said, looking after the prisoners is your responsibility.' Kurt rubbed his jaw while providing a rueful smile. 'And besides, he didn't let me speak for long enough to say we'd got two prisoners.'

'Still obliged you consulted me first, for once.' Shackleton gestured at the prisoners. 'But I've been talking to them while you were down there. I reckon you ought to hear what Nathaniel has to say.'

Kurt glanced at Nathaniel, then sneered.

'I ain't interested in hearing anything those two have to say.' Kurt raised his eyebrows. 'And I'm surprised at you. I thought you'd looked after prisoners for long enough not to believe their lies, especially when they're just days from the gallows.'

Shackleton's abashed frown suggested he thought it highly likely that Kurt was right.

Over the last two days Nathaniel had tried and failed several times to talk to them. Now that they'd used up nearly half of their allotted seven days following leads on Javier Rodriguez, all of which had led nowhere, he had hoped they were in just the right frame of mind to listen to his offer.

'Despite that, just listen to what he has to say,' Shackleton said. 'If you don't like it, I'll take them down to Mayor Maxwell.'

Kurt accepted these terms with a short nod, then stood over Nathaniel, who looked up at him and took a deep breath.

'It's like this,' Nathaniel said, 'I got wrongly accused of killing a man in Beaver Ridge jail and—'

'If that's what you're going to whine about,' Kurt snapped, 'I ain't wasting my time listening.'

'Then I'll give you the ending. I can take you to Javier Rodriguez.'

Kurt snorted. 'So what they say about you is true. You would sell anyone out to save yourself.'

'That ain't the way it is. Turner Jackson sold everyone out, including me. I was after him because only the truth from him can save me from the gallows.'

'All right, I believe you,' Kurt said in a sneering tone that suggested the opposite. 'So go on. Tell me where I can find Turner Jackson and Javier Rodriguez and I'll make him tell the truth and save your neck from a stretching.'

'I'll do that but I want to be there, helping to get them. That's part of the deal, or you won't ever find him.'

'As I thought. The deal is we free your bonds and then we ride around for days following your dubious directions while you look for a chance to run. That don't sound like a good deal to me.'

'Except I'll take you directly to him.'

Kurt pursed his lips, as if were taking this offer seriously.

'How far?'

Nathaniel sat back then raised his bound hands.

Kurt was just starting to shake his head when Shackleton spoke up.

'You'll have to give us something more than that, Nathaniel, as a show of faith, before we give you some leeway. Otherwise, I'll take you down to the mayor myself and he's determined to stretch someone's neck in front of the governor whether they were wrongly accused or not.'

'If you want something more, you'll have to free The Preacher too,' Nathaniel said, surprising himself with his comment. But now that he'd said it, it sounded right. The Preacher had saved his life, after all. 'He's the one who knows where Javier Rodriguez is.'

This comment made Kurt's eyes open wide then snap round to look at The Preacher.

'How can he possibly know that? He's been our prisoner for the last two days.'

'To be honest I don't exactly know how, but he

went to Baxter's Point without making any detours or even looking as if he was following a trail. I reckon he can do the same again.'

'But he's a babbling madman.'

'He ain't. The Preacher's intelligent. He's remembered every line in the Bible and can quote them all, but because he does that people think him a madman. So they ignore him and talk openly in front of him. I reckon he hears it all and remembers, and that means in jail he heard Javier's plans for what he'd do if he ever got free and that let him work out his weaknesses and motivations.'

Kurt shrugged and lowered his tone as if he were accepting this.

'Javier's motivation is simple. He's an evil varmint. I don't need no loco Bible man to tell me that.'

'Except it's more complicated than that. I can talk with him, sort of.'

'So you can talk with a madman.' Kurt snorted. 'That don't make me inclined to listen to you.'

With Kurt looking as if he'd heard enough, Nathaniel glanced at Shackleton. He gave an encouraging nod.

'Tell him the about the other man,' he said. 'That might interest him more.'

'There's also Turner Jackson,' Nathaniel said, 'the man I want. I saw him with Javier and I reckon he's wormed his way into Javier's confidence, just like he did with others before like Hiram Deeds. For the last year I shared a cell with Turner, so I know how he thinks. I can find him, and The Preacher knows how

Javier Rodriguez thinks and he can find him.'

'What do you reckon?' Shackleton asked, looking at Kurt. 'Three days riding with these two men with some hope, or three days riding without them with no hope?'

For a full minute Kurt didn't reply. Then, with a long sigh, he held out a hand for a knife.

'Here's the way it is,' he said. 'You both get to be free for the next three days. If you try to escape, I'll shoot you. The moment I think you're leading us in circles, I'll make you wish I'd taken you to the gallows. You don't get no weapon and once we have Javier Rodriguez, you both go straight to jail. Whether your help saves you from the gallows is up to the judge.'

'Obliged,' Nathaniel said as Kurt slit through his bonds, freeing his hands. 'A chance to help is all I asked for.'

Kurt moved on to The Preacher who had his hands already held out in his usual posture of praying. Kurt hesitated before he ripped through the rope.

'Not that anything will ever help to excuse this one before a judge.'

'The assembly must judge between him and the avenger of blood,' The Preacher said, 'Numbers thirty-five, verse twenty-four.'

Kurt considered this comment, shaking his head then looked at Nathaniel who, to avoid guessing what it meant, stood and paced around, enjoying the feeling of being free to move again.

But when he stopped he found that all three of those who would now be his companions in the search for the Gallows Gang were staring down at The Preacher with some trepidation.

'Just so I know,' Nathaniel said, joining Shackleton. 'What did The Preacher do to get sent to the gallows?'

Shackleton shivered then shook his head.

'If you ever want to have a good night's sleep again,' he said, 'don't ask me that.'

CHAPTER 13

'You lied,' Kurt snapped, summing up two days of increasing frustration with his simple comment.

Nathaniel looked down at the row of railroad men who were heading out of Chancer's Pass. He had to admit that in Kurt's position he'd have formed the same view.

'I didn't,' he said. 'There's still a high ridge for them to traverse before they reach Bear Creek.'

Kurt slapped to the ground the telescope with which he'd been surveying the scene and shook his head.

Nathaniel looked at Shackleton, hoping for support, but Shackleton's stern gaze showed that the small amount of faith he'd had in him when he'd accepted his offer had now gone. To Nathaniel's surprise that lack of faith hurt him.

'I agree with Kurt,' Shackleton said. 'Traipsing off after these men feels like wasted effort to me.'

'But we've come this far,' Nathaniel said. 'We need to see it through. If the payroll reaches the bank

116

safely, then hand us in, but not before.'

Shackleton looked at Elwood, who shook his head, then at the praying preacher who as usual appeared to be barely aware of what was happening around him, then at the sneering Kurt.

'I'm sorry,' he said, 'but this is where it ends for you, Nathaniel.'

Kurt grunted that he agreed. He picked up a coil of rope and waved it in Nathaniel's his face.

'Shackleton's got the right idea,' he said, 'so give it to me one last time and convince me or these will be your last ever moments of freedom.'

Nathaniel looked down into the pass at the receding men, then at Kurt.

'It's like this,' he said. 'I reckon The Preacher told me that Javier is trying to better his brother. Pablo never wanted to raid trains or steal the railroad payroll, so Javier will now do precisely that. Turner was serving life for various bank raids and his last failed ambush happened to be on a railroad payroll where he tried to blow up the pass they were going through. And two days ago a crate of dynamite got stolen from the train.'

'And so, based on the babbling of a madman and your hunch, you reckon Javier will blow up the pass?'

'That's what it amounts to.'

'That's a long way short,' Shackleton said, 'of you leading us directly to Javier Rodriguez like you promised. This is over.'

Shackleton gestured to Kurt to tie Nathaniel up, but Nathaniel edged back out of his range.

'How will you feel if you hear later that Javier did raid the payroll and you weren't there?'

Shackleton winced, then looked at Kurt, who shook his head, leaving Elwood to make the final decision. As usual Elwood didn't provide an immediate answer.

So, taking advantage of Elwood's rumination, Nathaniel swirled round to face The Preacher. He wanted to grab his shoulders and shake him until he gave him a straight answer. Any chance of their being treated leniently depended on their working out where Javier was. He wanted to impress that upon The Preacher, but he forced himself to accept that he would have to speak to The Preacher on his terms.

'An eye for an eye, a tooth for a tooth,' he said, starting with something they had always agreed upon.

'Exodus twenty-one, verse twenty-four,' The Preacher said.

'The brother casts his net wide,' Nathaniel said, uttering a few half-remembered words from one of The Preacher's many quotes which, he had decided, referred to Javier.

'All men lie in wait to shed blood,' The Preacher said, looking past his shoulder into the pass. 'Each hunts his brother with a net, Micah seven, verse two.'

'We shouldn't listen,' Elwood said, 'to any more of this nonsense.'

'Wait!' Nathaniel said. 'The Preacher's trying to tell us something. We're lying in wait and Pablo's brother is out there trying to kill the memory of his brother by raiding this—'

'I don't know who's worse,' Kurt snapped. 'Him for spouting this nonsense, or you for thinking it's not nonsense. For a start, Javier ain't hunting his brother and he hasn't got a net.'

'He's speaking in a different way from the way we do!' Nathaniel said, then forced himself to calm down before he spoke again to The Preacher. 'That hunt must end one day.'

The Preacher nodded. 'A mighty angel picked up a boulder the size of a large millstone and threw it into the sea, Revelation eighteen, verse twenty-one.'

'That's enough,' Kurt said, slapping a hand on Nathaniel's shoulder, but Nathaniel threw him off.

'And the ungodly deserved it,' Nathaniel urged.

'Saul went to the city of Amalek and set an ambush in the ravine, Samuel fifteen, verse five.'

This comment made Kurt stay his hand and look at The Preacher.

'Is he trying to tell us something, after all?' he asked.

Nathaniel ran all the comments through his mind, trying to think what he could say next to get something more meaningful from him. The Preacher had mentioned ambush, brother, ravine, boulder. . . .

He noted that The Preacher was still staring over his shoulder. He swirled round, then sat beside the man to see what it was that he had been staring at.

And there, 500 yards away at the mouth of the pass and less than half that distance from the receding line of men guarding the payroll was a massive boulder. It stood on an eroded outcrop of rock 200 feet above ground level, waiting for time and the elements to send it crashing down into the pass.

Nathaniel lunged for Kurt's telescope and put it to his eye. After several sweeps he sighted the boulder. Magnified, it appeared to be in an even more precarious position than before, somehow standing there with only a few feet of rock touching the ground. He couldn't see any sign of movement near it, but at the base he saw a flash of colour.

He strained his eyes, considering the small length of something that appeared to have been shoved beneath the boulder. Then he nodded to himself and thrust the telescope into Kurt's hands.

'I didn't lie and The Preacher doesn't babble,' he said.

Kurt took the telescope and peered at the boulder.

'What do you see?' Shackleton asked.

'Trouble,' Kurt murmured, then slapped the telescope closed and leapt to his feet. 'We have to warn everyone.'

Quickly they mounted up while Kurt told the others what he had seen. Then they headed down into the pass with Kurt leading, but he made no attempt to hide their presence.

'We going down there openly?' Shackleton asked.

Kurt slowed to answer. 'I ain't risking those men down there just to better our chances of catching Javier Rodriguez.'

Shackleton muttered that he agreed with this

sentiment. So, as they picked out their downward route, they hollered out to get the attention of the railroad men.

There were two wagons loaded down with crates with around a dozen men positioned before and behind them. The hindmost man dropped back to see who was approaching with his rifle already thrust out.

'We ain't trouble,' Shackleton shouted down when he was fifty yards from him. 'But you have to stop the wagons. The Gallows Gang are ahead.'

This revelation didn't perturb the man.

'We had men scouting ahead before we came through here,' he said. 'The Gallows Gang ain't here.'

'Yeah,' Shackleton said, drawing alongside Kurt. 'We saw how well those men searched and they didn't see us.'

The man narrowed his eyes. 'I recognize you. You're the men who let Javier Rodriguez escape in the first place. So how can *you* say we ain't good enough to do our job?'

'We ain't got time to argue.' Shackleton pointed ahead at the lead wagon then at the boulder just thirty yards ahead of it. 'There's dynamite under that boulder and it's going to blow at any moment.'

The man stayed staring at them for several seconds, then swirled round to look first at the wagon, then up at the boulder. He put his hands to his mouth, ready to holler ahead, but the words were drowned out when the promised explosion ripped out.

Rock and grit and smoke plumed up into the air behind the boulder before the dynamite achieved what centuries of the elements had failed to do. It toppled the boulder from its position to crash down a few feet, where it teetered, looking for a moment as if it might rock back on to its former pedestal. But the momentum from the blast was too great.

The boulder rolled, turned then went crashing down towards the wagon.

The men around the wagon shouted at each other, caught in a moment of indecision of trying to work out where the advancing boulder would come to rest. As the boulder rolled and thundered towards them they slowed then speeded, then slowed again until the wagon driver took matters into his own hands and cracked the reins sending the wagon on ahead.

This proved to be the right decision as with one last roll the boulder slammed down into the pass in an explosion of dirt and small rocks. Two men didn't make the right decision and disappeared beneath the boulder, and the noise and commotion spooked two horses enough to unseat their riders.

Then the shooting started.

The boulder had blocked the pass and Nathaniel judged that, aside from the wagon driver, only one other man was on the other side. Worse, all the gunfire was echoing beyond the boulder. On this side the men milled around the second wagon drawing Shackleton, Elwood and Kurt down to join them and debate their next actions.

For the first time Nathaniel found himself unguarded. He surveyed the scene, wondering how he could help again now that he'd been proved right.

Movement up the pass caught his eye and he looked up, seeing a man slipping away from a ledge close to where the boulder had stood. It was only a brief sighting and the man wouldn't have been visible from lower down in the pass, but Nathaniel had recognized Turner Jackson.

He jumped down from his horse, made his way along the side of the pass, then climbed upwards towards the ledge where he'd seen Turner. He heard shouting down below, but whether it was directed at him he didn't know.

More shooting was echoing beyond the boulder and as he reached higher ground he could see the wagon had halted. The driver was lying slumped and holed in his seat and the other man had crouched down behind the crates on the back, firing up into the pass.

Javier's men were moving down the pass to get closer to him. If he had a gun, Nathaniel reckoned he could pick them off, but as it was he could do nothing but seek out Turner.

He reached a point eight feet below the ledge where he stopped to consider his route. Then he scrambled up the first half. He paused for breath, then slapped a hand down on the top and moved to transfer his weight. Then a shadow loomed over him a moment before Turner came into view.

Turner stared down at him, smirking, then kicked out. With a jarring thud his boot landed squarely against Nathaniel's cheek and sent him tumbling backwards from the ledge.

He landed on his back and lay there, momentarily stunned. He could do nothing but look up as Turner drew his gun and aimed down at him. But then gunfire roared from below, kicking up pebbles around the edge of the ledge and making Turner flinch back out of view.

Nathaniel shook his head. Regaining his senses he then jumped to his feet and made for the ledge again. He climbed, then ventured a glance over the top to see Turner hurrying away.

Nathaniel rolled himself over on to the ledge, a stone breaking off in his grasp as he clawed his way to his knees.

Turner was twenty yards ahead with his back to him, running. Anger made Nathaniel grind his jaw and, taking this as his only chance, he drew back his hand then hurled the stone at Turner.

It flew with deadly accuracy heading straight for the centre of Turner's back, but a moment before the stone struck Turner slipped down to lower ground.

The stone still hit him with a glancing blow to the shoulder, making him reel round. Heartened now, Nathaniel scooped up another stone on the run and hurled it at Turner. The stone was smaller but this time it hit its target thudding into Turner's jaw and making him tumble from view.

Nathaniel ran on and reached the point where he'd hit Turner just in time to see him rolling and tumbling downwards. His limbs were waving as he fought to stop himself, but he continued to roll. If the fall didn't break his neck, Nathaniel saw that he was falling towards a point where Javier Rodriguez and the other members of the Gallows Gang were clambering over the wagon.

Javier was shouting out for everyone to leave as the railroad men were now slipping past the fallen boulder. Whether they'd wait for Turner, Nathaniel couldn't tell.

He looked for a way down, but then saw something that made him grin. Turner had dropped his gun. It lay five feet below him, and fifty feet below the gun the tumbling Turner was an easy target.

Nathaniel jumped down, having already decided that as long as he managed to wound Turner, Javier would have to leave him. He reached out, his fingers touching the cold metal, when a voice rang out behind him.

'Don't move, Nathaniel McBain.'

Nathaniel stilled his hand, then glanced back to see that Kurt was walking towards him with his gun trained on him.

'Turner's down there,' Nathaniel said. 'He knows I'm innocent. I just want t—'

'You don't want to do nothing, Nathaniel. You're a prisoner and a prisoner with a gun is a dead man.'

CHAPTER 14

Javier Rodriguez had stolen half the railroad payroll.

That was the stark news that greeted Nathaniel when Kurt had escorted him down into the pass. Turner Jackson had also got away and now the railroad men were in pursuit, leaving Kurt and Shackleton behind.

Worse news was to follow when Shackleton reported the reason why Kurt had been so determined not to let Nathaniel take the gun.

'The Preacher's gone,' he said.

'He can't have got far,' Nathaniel said.

'How do you know that?' Kurt asked, sneering. 'Did he tell you that in one of his Bible quotes when you were plotting to escape?'

Nathaniel tried to explain that this wasn't the case but neither man would listen to him. When Elwood returned from the other side of the boulder, he confirmed the truth.

'The Preacher,' he said, 'rode off after Javier Rodriguez.'

'That'll be to get his revenge on him like I said,' Nathaniel said. 'But listen to me. I can work out how to find him.'

'We've seen his version of revenge back at Wilson's Crossing,' Kurt said, 'and you ain't got no way of finding him.'

'Except I have,' Nathaniel said. 'I've been thinking and I reckon the reason he'll talk to me is that he took me under the water with him. He thinks he's baptized me and I'm now his disciple.'

That turned out to be the worst musing he could have spoken aloud as everyone curled their lips with disgust, then turned their backs on him.

For the next fifteen minutes the surviving men discussed their next actions. Half of the railroad men were in pursuit of Javier, and Kurt and Shackleton reckoned they'd let them get on with the job while they scouted around to see what else they could learn in the pass.

When they returned their mood hadn't lightened. None of the Gallows Gang had been killed, but five railroad men were either dead or unaccounted for.

The men in Shackleton's group were in a sombre mood when they left the railroad men to find their own route out of the pass with the second wagon. They found that Javier's trail was an easy one to follow and was broadly towards Bear Creek.

As they rode Nathaniel tried to think what he could say to change their minds. He had correctly worked out where the raid would take place and he'd so nearly captured Turner.

But none of the men appeared interested in viewing his actions favourably after he'd run away from them, tried to get a gun and, most damning, after The Preacher had taken advantage of the situation to escape.

Nobody's mood had lightened when an hour later they approached a river and Elwood reported that he could see something untoward ahead.

They dismounted to take in the surroundings, then Kurt and Shackleton moved on ahead, leaving Nathaniel with Elwood. The two men disappeared into a copse of trees, emerging two minutes later with their faces set even more grimly than before.

Elwood urged Nathaniel to move on, letting him see that they'd come across the aftermath of a pitched battle.

The wagon lay on its side, but the crates containing the payroll had gone. The bodies of the railroad men lay scattered around the wagon. Most had taken cover behind the wagon, not that that had done them any good, and the two who hadn't been shot had suffered the trademark fate of the Gallows Gang.

Their bodies dangled from a tree. While Elwood cut them down Kurt and Shackleton stared at Nathaniel as if he were to blame for this atrocity.

'Not like the sight, then, Nathaniel?' Kurt said. 'That's what you'll be getting tomorrow night.'

'Unless you can find Javier Rodriguez first,' Nathaniel said, reckoning this would be his last opportunity to talk them round. 'And I can—'

'I don't want to hear it,' Kurt said. 'We've got a

trail to follow and we don't need you no more.'

Kurt looked at Shackleton who nodded, then gestured to Elwood.

'Elwood,' Shackleton said, 'take him back to Bear Creek, then try to catch up with us.'

'Sure will and good luck,' Elwood said, placing a hand on Nathaniel's back to usher him back to his horse.

'That goes for me too,' Nathaniel said, looking at Shackleton as he judged him to be the most amenable of the men as regarded listening to him. 'I did my best back there in the pass and if you can capture Turner alive, you'll get to hear the truth that I'm not the man everyone reckons I am.'

Shackleton gave him a brief look that said he sympathized but that he was no longer prepared to listen. But even his attitude hardened when Kurt called him over to look at the cut-down bodies. Kurt held up a screwed-up piece of paper in one hand as he bent to remove a second piece of paper from the mouth of one of the bodies.

'This is a change,' Shackleton said.

'Yeah,' Kurt said, 'both bodies had their mouths filled with paper and a message, courtesy of The Preacher.'

Kurt held out the sheets for Shackleton to read what had been written on them. Then both men shook their heads as Kurt screwed them up.

'What do they say?' Nathaniel called out but Kurt didn't reply other than to walk over and hurl the balls of paper at him. With his hands tied behind his back the paper rebounded from his chest and dropped to the ground.

'More babbling from your friend.'

'Yeah, but what do they say? It might be a clue. The Preacher might have worked out where Javier is going, or he might—'

'Show him, Shackleton,' Kurt said. 'I can't bear to talk to him no more.'

Shackleton picked up the papers, smoothed them out, then held them up before Nathaniel's face.

'Anyone who looks at a woman lustfully has already committed adultery with her in his heart, Matthew five, verse twenty-eight,' Nathaniel said, reading aloud. Then he moved on to the second one. 'If a man marries his brother's wife, it is an act of impurity, Leviticus twenty, verse twenty-one.'

'You want to make one last guess what that means before Elwood takes you back to Bear Creek?'

'Did Pablo or Javier have a wife?'

'Nope, and that was your only guess.'

'Wait! I can't think what it means right now, but The Preacher wants his revenge on Javier after he left us to die. So I reckon he's leaving us clues as to where we can find him, if we can only figure them out.'

Shackleton shook his head. 'You've spent too much time with The Preacher. You're starting to babble as much he did.'

'You can't go!' Javier snapped.

'We've got thousands of dollars here,' Chester

said. 'That's good enough for us.'

'Yeah,' William said, nodding. 'When we were heading for the gallows, this money was more than I could ever have dreamed of.'

'Your dreams,' Javier said, 'are as limited as Pablo's were. This is just the start. We can blaze a trail. We can become legend.'

'You can do that,' Chester said. 'We just want the money.'

Javier glared at Chester and William in turn, his thunderous expression looking as if he was preparing himself to strangle both men with his bare hands. Accordingly they both backed away a pace, their hands drifting towards their holsters, but then Javier pointed over their shoulders.

'Go if you ain't got the guts to stay!' he snapped, turning his back on them.

He stood, stooped and grinding his teeth, while Chester and William mounted up and left. Only when the hoofbeats had receded into the distance did he raise his head to consider what was left of the Gallows Gang.

He'd had high hopes of what they could achieve and now in less than a week only Aaron and Turner were left.

'I can go and get the money back,' Turner said, leaning towards him and winking.

'No,' Javier said. 'We don't need them or their money to finish what I started.'

'That mean you'll raid the bank?' Turner said, rubbing his hands with glee.

'No,' Javier said, brightening, 'I have something far more important than that in mind.'

'You've got a visitor,' Deputy Albright said, peering at Nathaniel through the cell bars.

'Shackleton? Elwood? Kurt?' Nathaniel asked, but the deputy shook his head.

'Nope. The mayor.' Albright headed away from the cell.

While keys rattled and a door clanged Nathaniel stared at a stretch of mildew on his cell wall as he had been doing for the last few hours, trying to work out what The Preacher had meant. He felt as if he were close to understanding it, but he couldn't quite connect all the details together.

'The Gallows Gang,' Mayor Maxwell said when he reached his cell. 'You ain't looking so dangerous now you're back where you belong.'

With nothing else to occupy his mind Nathaniel swung his legs down to the floor and paced across the cell to face his visitor.

'I'm not dangerous. I never was a member of the Gallows Gang and I reckon with more time I might even be able to help you find them.'

Mayor Maxwell nodded slowly. 'I'd heard you'd sold out the prisoners back in Beaver Ridge.'

'That ain't the way it was.'

'Let's save time by presuming it was. Governor Stuart will want to see someone hang tomorrow, but it doesn't have to be you.' Mayor Maxwell ran a finger down a bar. 'Tell me where I can find Javier

Rodriguez and you won't join him.'

Nathaniel considered blurting out his whole story, but decided it wasn't worth the effort. Mayor Maxwell wanted only one thing, and he couldn't provide it, yet.

'I don't know his exact location, but the men who found me are on his tail. I'm sure they'll get him. From what I saw and heard, Javier Rodriguez ain't as invincible as everyone reckons he is.'

Mayor Maxwell slapped a bar. 'Him and his brother were the worst outlaws this county's ever known.'

Nathaniel shook his head. If the story he'd pieced together from The Preacher was right, Javier was embarking on a plan to better his brother's exploits. Yet Javier's exploits were of the kind he'd have expected Pablo to have committed to get such a bad reputation. As far as he could tell, the Pablo Rodriguez Gang had been just a bunch of trouble-makers and not at all like the ruthless outlaw band the Gallows Gang had become.

'What did they do to become so hated?' he asked.

'They terrorized this town for nigh on a year, shooting men who got in their way, raping women who tried to stay out of their way.'

Mayor Maxwell grabbed the bars so tightly the knuckles whitened, his anger out of proportion to how Nathaniel thought he should react.

'Did they shoot any men, or rape any women in particular?' he asked, the hint of an idea coming to him.

'Narcissa,' Mayor Maxwell snapped, 'my only daughter.'

'Javier or Pablo?'

'Both, either, I don't know.'

'You mean she's so traumatized she can't remember?'

'Or is protecting . . . I don't know. She won't say but I want Javier to pay like Pablo did.' Mayor Maxwell pointed a firm finger at him. 'So do you know anything or am I wasting my time talking to you?'

Nathaniel was minded to say he could help him, but the anger in Maxwell's eyes suggested it'd fall on deaf ears, so he shook his head.

When the mayor had taken his leave of him, Nathaniel rolled back down on to his cot and resumed his inspection of the mildew patch. This time it felt as though the extra information the mayor had imparted was enough to put the answers he was looking for all together.

The Pablo Rodriguez gang were a band of troublemakers who had committed the worst possible crime when they'd involved the mayor's family, even if the mayor's cryptic comment suggested that that crime might not have been quite what it seemed. . . .

An hour later, when Deputy Albright brought him his evening meal, he stood up and put on his most reasonable voice.

'I have a message for Marshal Kurt McLynn and Shackleton Frost,' he said.

'I ain't no messenger,' Albright muttered.

'They'll come to town before Governor Stuart arrives and I'm sure they'll make it worth your while.' Nathaniel raised his voice as Albright turned away. 'Tell them – this time I know where he is, I really do.'

'I'll be sure to let them know,' Albright called over his shoulder in a dismissive manner that said he'd already forgotten the message.

CHAPTER 15

Shackleton hit the ground and rolled, letting the slug whine over his tumbling form, then he scrambled into hiding behind the only available cover, a mound.

Kurt followed him behind the mound, diving full length as a volley of gunshots whistled overhead.

'Well,' he said, shuffling round to lie beside him, 'it appears we found 'em.'

Shackleton risked looking up to see that their assailants had also gone to ground in a hollow twenty yards away.

'Some of 'em,' he said. 'There's just two men out there and neither of them is Javier Rodriguez.'

'But we're picking them off now.' Kurt drew his gun and crawled closer to the top of the mound. He lay quietly for several seconds, then took a deep breath and turned to Shackleton. 'So before we do this, I just want to say, you and Elwood have done well this last week.'

'We spent a whole week failing to find Javier,' Shackleton said.

'I know, but you learn a lot about a man when you ride with him for a week and I reckon you both did everything you possibly could do to get him.' Kurt sighed. 'If we could start again back at Beaver Ridge jail, I reckon I'd listen to what you had to say.'

Shackleton reckoned that was the nearest he would get to an apology for having ignored his recommendations. He might have made a magnanimous comment of his own, but the memory of Barney's death was still too recent.

'Let's not get all misty-eyed,' he said. 'We've got two outlaws to take.'

Kurt nodded. Then, after a brief exchange of views on tactics they split up. Shackleton rolled away from the hollow to lie flat while Kurt went the other way and, doubled over, made his way towards the hollow where the outlaws had gone to ground.

He'd covered half the distance when one of them risked looking up with his gun aimed squarely at the mound, but then he found that his targets had moved. He started to swing the gun to the side, but Shackleton's low shot winged along just inches off the ground and sliced through his hat.

The man flopped to lie flat and when Kurt put a second bullet in him the body merely twitched, lifelessly.

'You over there,' Kurt shouted, gesturing at Shackleton to be ready. 'We only want Javier Rodriguez. Tell us where he is and you can go free.'

'I don't believe you,' a voice shouted from the hollow.

'What you got to lose?'

'All right. Javier Rodriguez ain't here. He's got some big plan. Something important to him.'

'Not good enough. You get to die.'

Then Kurt threw himself to the side to move away from the last place he'd spoken. Sure enough the man bobbed up, but his gun homed in on Shackleton.

Staring straight down the barrel of a gun over twenty yards Shackleton fired but the man was still moving and his shot buried itself in the dirt two feet away from his target.

Shackleton winced, but then another shot rang out and to his relief Shackleton saw Kurt's deadly slug to the chest make the man roll away. Then Kurt was on his feet and running for his assailant, shooting on the run. This time Shackleton didn't complain when he didn't try to take the man prisoner.

'Obliged,' he said when he joined Kurt. 'You saved my life there.'

'We saved each other's lives,' Kurt said, standing over the dead bodies. 'But even if we've got another two, we're down to the last few hours to save our careers.'

'You don't think two more bodies will satisfy Mayor Maxwell?'

'Nope.'

'Then you got any idea what Javier's last big plan could be?'

Kurt shook his head. 'Nope to that too. We have no hope.'

'We have.' Shackleton remembered something his father had once said to him. 'Those who plot evil go astray. Those who plan what is good find success.'

Kurt narrowed his eyes. 'That some sort of biblical quotation?'

'I reckon so.'

Kurt sighed. 'And just when we were starting to get on so well.'

The shadows were getting longer, shrouding the gallows in gloom.

Nathaniel tried to avoid looking at them but with nothing else to occupy his mind he frequently found himself jumping up to look through the small grille at the platform they'd obligingly built outside the jailhouse.

If nobody responded to his message in the next hour, his would be the only neck anyone would see stretched. Every time Deputy Albright had checked on him he'd urged him to get his message out and had even shouted through the grille at passers-by, but nobody had showed.

He was embarking on another round of pacing his cell when he heard approaching footfalls. He threw himself to the bars and pressed his face between them.

'You've got to get word to Shackleton,' he demanded. 'It's not just my life that depends on it.'

'He did,' Shackleton said, pacing into view.

Nathaniel looked skyward, relief overcoming him for a moment.

'You came,' he said when he felt composed enough to talk.

'Don't get too excited. We didn't exactly have much of a choice.'

'No luck finding Javier, then?'

'Nope. We followed every trail we could find, but none of them led to Javier or even your friend The Preacher. So in the end we had to admit defeat. Kurt's getting a few drinks inside him before he hands in his star, and I might join him before I tell Governor Bradbury want I think of him.'

'It doesn't have to end that way.'

'Governor Stuart's train is due in five minutes. If we couldn't find Javier in a week, there ain't much hope we can do in that time.'

'But there is time. I wasn't lying. I know where Javier is.'

'So you reckon Javier is in town?' Shackleton mused.

'No guessing. Do we have a deal?'

Shackleton snorted. 'I figured there'd be a deal, so Elwood is buying his old friend Deputy Albright a drink and generally distracting him. Spell it out.'

'It's like this: I can't trust this to others. Turner Jackson is the only man who knows the truth and can save me from the gallows. I have to find him and make him talk. Let me out of here and I'll lead you to him, and to Javier.'

'And if we fail?'

140

'That won't happen, but if I'm wrong. . . .' Nathaniel sighed. 'I won't lie to you. I will try to run, but I won't harm nobody.'

Shackleton raised a key and dangled it on an outstretched finger.

'If you'd said you'd give yourself in, I'd have walked away, but I'll trust you enough to accept that. So now trust me and I'll put this key in the lock. Where is Javier?'

Nathaniel considered for a moment then leaned forward.

'It's not a where, but a who.'

CHAPTER 16

'This is all very interesting,' Governor Stuart said, his voice muffled by the kerchief he held over his mouth as he considered Mitch Cartwright's body, 'but I came to see an execution, not bodies.'

Mayor Maxwell wafted away a fly and forced himself to move down the line.

'I thought it important you saw the whole Gallows Gang. So you knew all about the good work we've been doing.'

Two of the governor's aides had already passed up the opportunity for this examination of the men they'd brought to justice and the third had merely passed out. The governor was built of sterner stuff, something Mayor Maxwell had counted on when he'd set out to buy himself a few more minutes' leeway before delivering the bad news.

Stuart harrumphed, but he moved on to consider the next bloated corpse, the passage of a week ensuring that even Casey Dawson's family wouldn't recognize him.

'This is good work.' He looked at the next body, which, as it had come from the battle in Devil's Canyon was in an even worse state. 'But now that I've seen them, get these men buried and stop them stinking up the town.'

'We'll do that, Governor.'

'And show me to Javier Rodriguez.' The governor turned to the door and marched purposefully outside.

'Ah,' Mayor Maxwell said. 'I thought that first I could interest you in something to eat and drink with my only daughter.'

'No more delays, Maxwell.'

Mayor Maxwell let his shoulders slump. 'That's a pity. My daughter was looking forward to spending a few minutes with you, especially after she suffered such a traumatic experience recently. . . .'

Stuart's glare said he knew Mayor Maxwell was applying emotional blackmail as well as wasting his time, but the consummate politician nodded.

'I'd be delighted to meet your daughter.' Stuart waited until Mayor Maxwell smiled. 'But this is the last delay.'

'Of course,' Mayor Maxwell said, looking around. 'Now where is Narcissa? She should be back by now.'

'You!' Narcissa Maxwell exclaimed.

Javier Rodriguez stepped out from the confines of the mercantile.

'I said I'd come.'

'But Father's got men looking out for you, lots of them.'

143

'That doesn't concern me. I have enough money to leave for Mexico.'

'I never thought you were serious about that,' she said, putting a hand to her heart.

'Of course I was. It's far enough away for a new life, for all of us.' Javier gestured at Turner and Aaron as they emerged from their hiding-places around the store. The sight made Narcissa gulp.

'With these men?'

'They're not as unfriendly as they look. We all just want a second chance, don't we?'

Aaron provided a supportive grunt, but Turner didn't.

'We came back here for a woman?' he muttered.

'Yeah.'

'But you said back in the trading post that we didn't take women with us, unlike Pablo.'

The mention of Pablo made Javier snort and advance on Turner.

'Don't ever question my orders again.'

'I'm not,' Turner murmured, backing away a pace. 'You said you'd brought us here for something even more important than the bank.'

'Quit talking about the bank! This is more important and you've made a big mistake, Turner. You showed your hand too early. You won't take over from me.'

'I never wanted to do that and besides, look at us, there's nothing to take over.'

Javier dismissed that matter with a wave of the hand.

'Don't think I don't know what you did to Mitch.'

Turner gulped. 'I didn't kill him, and I don't want to take over.'

Javier considered Turner's darting eyes, then nodded.

'You don't. That's not the way you operate. On your own you're nothing, but you wheedle and plot against others until you get what you want, but no more.' Javier pointed at him. 'I know who you are, Turner Jackson. I'm watching you. The moment you stop being useful to me, I'll kill you, understand?'

'Yeah,' Turner murmured, lowering his head.

Javier glared at him for a moment longer then turned and converted his harsh expression to a soft smile as he faced Narcissa.

'So are you coming with me?' he asked.

'Of course,' she said.

She moved towards the door, but Javier thrust out a hand to grab her arm and squeezed.

'Tell me what I want to hear first.'

'You're hurting me.'

'I'd never do that. Just say it.'

She firmed her jaw to avoid showing she was in pain, then nodded.

'Pablo meant nothing to me.'

'You'd have never left with him, would you?'

'He never asked.' She squealed when Javier tightened his grip. 'But if he had, I wouldn't have left town for him, only you.'

'And you didn't play us off against each other?'

Narcissa fluttered her eyelashes, making Javier

smile. He released his hand, letting her come up to him and throw her hands around his neck.

'It was only ever you,' she said. 'Pablo never had the guts to do any of the things you've done. Only you could impress me.'

'They're inside,' Elwood said when he'd hurried back into hiding behind the cluster of barrels facing the mercantile. 'They'll come out any moment now.'

Kurt raised his eyebrows, surprised that Nathaniel's information had proved to be correct. Nathaniel limited himself to sighing with relief, but Shackleton felt a need to say something.

'I have to say,' he said, looking at Kurt, 'I really am obliged to you for saving my life earlier, and I reckon you did well this last week, too.'

'Glad we got ourselves an understanding,' Kurt said, 'eventually.'

'We have. You're a better lawman than I gave you credit for. You worked out that what happened to Narcissa wasn't what it seemed. If I had listened to you, we'd have probably found Javier a whole lot faster.'

Kurt shrugged. 'And if I had listened to you, Javier would probably never have got away in the first place. But, like you said to me earlier, this ain't the time to get all misty-eyed.'

Shackleton snorted in agreement. Then they settled down to wait.

Presently a man sidled out of the mercantile. Nathaniel murmured that he was Aaron, one of the escaped prisoners.

Aaron paced out into the road while glancing around and taking in the lack of people. Everyone in town who was out had congregated around the gallows either to witness the grisly event or to see Governor Stuart.

'You can come out,' he shouted inside, and Javier emerged with a smiling Narcissa on his arm.

'You were right,' Shackleton whispered to Nathaniel. 'She don't look like she's being kidnapped.'

'Although she'll claim that's what did happen later,' Nathaniel whispered, 'when she finds out that consorting with outlaws ain't as exciting as she thought it'd be.'

Shackleton nodded, then glanced at Kurt and Elwood to co-ordinate their attack. Nathaniel started to say that Turner was unaccounted for, but by then the others had slapped their guns down on the top of the barrels.

Their motion alerted Javier and he pushed Narcissa away with one hand while throwing his other hand to his gun. He crouched and fired, but even his lightning speed wasn't fast enough to draw and aim accurately and his twin slugs clattered uselessly into the barrels.

The three armed men he faced fired only two shots each in response but they all found a target. Three bullets tore into Javier's body, making him spin away. The other slugs sent Aaron flying back-wards through the window.

The gunfire was still reverberating when Nathaniel leapt to his feet and ran for the mercantile. Shackleton was close on his heels while Kurt headed for Javier and Elwood ran for Narcissa, who decided that this rapid turn of events provided her with the appropriate opportunity to faint.

Nathaniel leapt on to the boardwalk and moved for the door, but then flinched back when a slug tore splinters from the doorjamb. He turned at the hip, making his instinctive movement before he remembered he was unarmed. He saw the wounded Javier in the road looking at him, his shaking arm trying to steady his gun hand, but before Nathaniel could dive away Kurt leapt on Javier and pinned him to the ground.

Then Nathaniel ran through the door with his head down.

Aaron was still moving below the window, his gun hand rising, but Shackleton followed Nathaniel inside and blasted lead into him, making him twitch then flop.

'Obliged,' Nathaniel said, seeing the back door swinging open.

He ran for the door as Shackleton and Elwood shouted to each other confirming that the situation outside was under control. This time he was more cautious and darted his head out of the door, then drew it back in. His glance took in the form of a man running away – Turner Jackson.

Nathaniel pressed himself to the doorjamb, preparing himself to leap out and chase the fleeing

148

man, but then cold metal thrust into his neck. He turned to see that Shackleton had his gun on him.

'I ain't saying you were about to run,' he said, 'but I am saying you won't.'

'I wasn't. Turner's out there.'

Shackleton winced, then raised his gun, letting Nathaniel swing outside. But the delay in moving out had been too long.

Turner had gone.

'I have had enough of these delays,' Governor Stuart said. 'Show me Javier Rodriguez now or I will leave and never return.'

Mayor Maxwell mopped his brow while staring down the road.

'Yes, but—'

'And don't say you're worried about that gunfire. I don't care about it. The only thing I care about is seeing Javier Rodriguez getting justice.'

Mayor Maxwell nodded, accepting that his career was about to end while consoling himself with the thought that his wouldn't be the only one. But a residual element of interest in the welfare of his town made him look down the road, wondering what trouble was going on.

'I have to admit,' he murmured as the men he'd sent to investigate emerged from the corner beyond the mercantile. 'There's been a problem.'

'Then sort it out, man. I didn't come here for no lawyers to waste my time by delaying Javier's execution.'

'It's not lawyers, so it'll be a short delay, I'm sure, but a delay in delivering justice to Javier Rodriguez is inevitable.'

'Why?'

To avoid looking at the glaring governor, Mayor Maxwell looked at the advancing phalanx of men.

Marshal Kurt McLynn was amongst them, as was Shackleton Frost. They were escorting someone, but with so many people around him, Maxwell couldn't see who. Whoever it was was badly wounded and had to be held up by two men. . . .

Then he saw who it was.

'Because,' he said, licking his lips, 'you have to congratulate the men who brought him to justice first, the two men I rank above any others I know.'

CHAPTER 17

Nathaniel stood at the back of the group of men around the gallows with Shackleton and Elwood guarding him, while Mayor Maxwell and Governor Stuart were busily discussing Javier Rodriguez and his impending demise.

Kurt was trying to get a word in to mention that there would be only one person getting on the gallows. Nathaniel could do nothing but hope that Maxwell's good mood meant he would be willing to listen to sense.

Nathaniel was doing his best to avoid looking at the noose. So he was the only one looking down the road when a wagon emerged from the edge of town, then came hurtling towards them, taking a reckless path that scattered people before it.

'What in tarnation is the damn fool doing?' Maxwell demanded when the rising hubbub drew his attention, but his men had already provided their own answer as they closed ranks around Javier Rodriguez.

Whether Javier had been the man's target or not Nathaniel couldn't tell, but the volume of people in front of the driver made him veer away. Then he set a course towards the bank at the opposite end of town.

As the wagon turned, Nathaniel got a clear view of the driver.

'Turner Jackson,' he muttered. He looked at Shackleton, who held his hands high, releasing him.

'Let's get him this time,' Shackleton said, 'together.'

'Obliged,' Nathaniel said, then set off.

He'd managed only a few paces before someone shouted out that their prisoner was getting away. Orders ripped out to cut him off.

Two guards moved in from either side, but Shackleton stopped and remonstrated with them. Then Elwood and Kurt stepped forward, but by then Nathaniel had barged his way free of the milling people.

Turner was heading the wagon down the road fifty yards ahead of him and so Nathaniel looked for a free horse. He couldn't see one, so he had no choice but to break into a run. He'd covered only a few paces before pounding footfalls sounded. Then a man ran into him, knocking him to the ground.

He rolled and came up facing his assailant, then shoved him away. Behind the man others were moving to recapture him but Kurt and Elwood were taking them on and blocking their route.

Shackleton advanced on Nathaniel's assailant and

slapped a hand on his shoulder, then swung him round and grounded him with an uppercut to the chin. Even before he'd hit the ground another man leapt on Shackleton's back and wrestled him to the ground.

Shackleton fought his way out of the man's grip for a moment. With his free hand he drew his gun and underhanded it to Nathaniel.

'Get him,' he shouted, then threw the man off his back. He swung round to take on the next two men trying to run Nathaniel down.

Nathaniel turned to find the delay had let Turner get further away from him. He was now over one hundred yards down the road. With a forlorn feeling overcoming him, he sprinted after his quarry, seeing him get further away with every pace he took. Nathaniel followed, hoping that maybe Turner would turn or slow down so that he could get a clear shot at him.

The last building to pass before Turner reached the bank was the church. He swung the wagon to the side, passing close by it as he started a wide turn. The movement slowed the wagon down, cheering Nathaniel into running faster.

Then he saw that someone was on the church roof. The tall figure emerged over the ridge, then strode down at speed without care for his safety.

'The Preacher,' Nathaniel murmured to himself.

The Preacher reached the edge of the roof just as Turner passed beneath him. Without breaking his stride he stepped off the roof.

Below, Turner flinched, catching sight of The Preacher's shadow at the last moment, but by then The Preacher had landed on the back of the wagon. He bent his knees to steady himself, then lunged forward. He grabbed Turner around the neck and tugged backwards.

The reins slipped from Turner's grip and the already slowing wagon slewed across the road before halting. Heartened now, Nathaniel hurried on, seeing The Preacher and Turner struggling.

The Preacher kept Turner sitting forward while he stayed behind him, trying to pull him into the back of the wagon, but Turner tore himself free, then moved for his gun.

Nathaniel skidded to a halt, took aim past the figure of The Preacher, then fired. He only had the side of Turner's body to aim at but his shot ripped into Turner's shoulder, knocking him from view.

The Preacher swung over into the seat, then bore down on Turner's body as Nathaniel broke into a run, pounding across the ground over the last twenty yards. He slipped around the side of the wagon.

As it had come to a halt lengthways across the road, he could see that the guards had broken away from his helpers and were now running down the road towards him.

Then he looked to the wagon where, one-handed, Turner was keeping The Preacher off him. The Preacher was now clawing for the reins and that gave Turner enough leeway to push him away. He still had a hold of his gun and he swung it round, aiming to shoot The Preacher in the side, but Nathaniel halted him with a strident cry.

'Don't shoot or you're a dead man,' he demanded.

Turner looked to the side to consider Nathaniel and shook his head.

'You won't shoot me. I'm the only person who can let you escape the gallows.' He glanced down the road. 'And I reckon you'll be getting escorted there any second now.'

From the corner of his eye, Nathaniel saw the mayor's men hurrying towards him, now just thirty yards away. He also heard the fateful fizzing noise he'd heard a week ago back in the cage. That led him to look at the crates on the back of the wagon and the wording on the side of the nearest crate drew his eye. . . .

'You got plenty wrong, Turner,' he said.

He fired, blasting Turner between the eyes and kicking him out of his seat. Then he jumped on to the wagon to join The Preacher.

'Let's get this wagon out of town,' he shouted.

The Preacher wasted no time in getting a firm grip of the reins. While he shook them, getting the wagon moving, Nathaniel swung round in his seat to face the advancing pursuers.

'Get back!' he shouted. 'The wagon's loaded down with dynamite, and it's going to blow at any moment.'

Half the men stopped. The other half carried on running, then slowed to a halt when they got close

155

enough to see the wording on the crates.

When Nathaniel turned, they were swinging past the bank as The Preacher headed the wagon towards the edge of town. A few people were ahead of them, but the cries of alarm coming from behind the wagon was encouraging them to scurry into hiding.

'How long do you reckon we've got before this wagon blows sky high?' Nathaniel asked.

'In the beginning God created the heavens and the earth,' The Preacher said.

'That soon,' Nathaniel murmured, remembering the last time he'd heard this quote.

'The earth was formless and empty, darkness was over the surface of the deep.'

Nathaniel grabbed The Preacher's shoulder.

'This is far enough. We have to jump.'

The Preacher ignored him. 'The Spirit of God was hovering over the waters. And God said . . .'

The Preacher released a hand from the reins and shoved Nathaniel's shoulder, tipping him backwards from the seat.

Nathaniel rolled once, then hit the ground. He moved to get up, seeing the wagon now trundling beyond the edge of town, The Preacher riding it off into clear space.

Over the rattling of the wagon wheels Nathaniel heard The Preacher shout out.

'Let there be light!' he cried, raising his hands to the heavens.

Then Nathaniel just had time to turn his back before the dynamite exploded.

Nathaniel dropped to the ground, his hands rising to cover his head as wood and stones hurtled by him. Long moments passed while Nathaniel could only wait. Then all he could do was stand and turn and hope that maybe The Preacher had leapt clear. But there was no sign of him.

'And there was light,' Nathaniel said, making his slow way towards the smoking crater.

CHAPTER 18

'And so,' Judge Matthews said, summing up, 'I now have a decision to make as to your fate, Nathaniel McBain. On the one hand you had a key role in bringing Javier Rodriguez to justice and you saved many lives when you took the dynamite out of town. On the other hand I convicted you for killing Ramsey Carr, and you were implicated in the deaths of four innocent people at Wilson's Crossing. What have you got to say about that?'

'If I could have avoided killing Turner Jackson so that he could talk I would have,' Nathaniel said, 'but as I had to save lives, I had no choice. That means I can't prove anything about Ramsey Carr now. As for what happened at Wilson's Crossing: I feel sorry for those people, but The Preacher did that and as you saw, he was an odd man seeking salvation in a misguided way.'

'That is one way of looking at it, but I agree that The Preacher was to blame, not you.' Judge Matthews reached over for a sheet of paper. 'And it appears I have some useful new information about Turner's role in the murder of Ramsey Carr. Marshal Kurt McLynn overheard you speaking with Turner in Chancer's Pass and he heard Turner say, and I quote: "I killed Ramsey Carr and nobody but you knows that. I laugh when I think about how you, an innocent man, will go to the gallows for something that I, and only I, did." An interesting speech for him to make, I'm sure you'll agree, when he was fighting for his life in the middle of an ambush.'

Judge Matthews paused while subdued coughing echoed around the courtroom, then looked across the room at Kurt, who was wisely looking elsewhere.

'And so,' Judge Matthews continued, 'it would appear that based on everything I have heard I must reconsider my earlier judgement.'

'Thank you,' Nathaniel said, then gulped with relief.

'But I am also mindful of the fact that I could be wrong again. So my judgement is that I will send you back to Beaver Ridge and delay your appointment with the gallows for a year and a day. If in that time you act responsibly, you will be a free man.'

Judge Matthews raised his eyebrows, inviting Nathaniel to speak.

'I accept your judgement,' Nathaniel said, 'but plenty of prisoners think I sold them out in Beaver Ridge. It might be better for everyone's sake to send me somewhere else.'

'That isn't possible. It is an essential requirement of your sentence that you will go to Beaver Ridge, then come back here.' The judge waved his hand back and forth. 'Then go back to Beaver Ridge, then go to—'

'I don't understand.'

Judge Matthews smiled as he peered at him.

'Shackleton Frost has offered to oversee the final stages of your rehabilitation and make sure you are a changed man. He lost a good man back in Devil's Canyon and he has kindly agreed that you should take over that man's duties. Of course if you would prefer to go back to jail instead of escorting prisoners. . . .'

'No,' Nathaniel blurted. 'That kind of work sounds just fine.'

He looked over towards Shackleton, then Kurt. He smiled before turning back to face the judge.

'May the grace of the Lord Jesus be with God's people,' Judge Matthews said as he raised his gavel to commit him to being a free man.

Nathaniel nodded. 'Revelation twenty-two, verse twenty-one.'

u
3(

2

2